The CHARLIE CHAPLIN Book

Ten Stories Adapted from Classic Shorts

ROBERT KEENE THOMPSON

DOVER PUBLICATIONS, INC.
MINEOLA, NEW YORK

Bibliographical Note

This Dover edition, first published in 2016, is a newly reset, unabridged republication of the work originally published by Street & Smith Publishers, New York, in 1915.

Library of Congress Cataloging-in-Publication Data

Names: Thompson, Robert Keene, 1885–1937, author.
Title: The Charlie Chaplin book : ten stories adapted from classic shorts / Robert Keene Thompson.
Description: Mineola, New York : Dover Publications, 2016. | "This Dover edition, first published in 2016, is a newly reset, unabridged republication of the work originally published by Street & Smith Publishers, New York, in 1915."
Identifiers: LCCN 2016007117| ISBN 9780486806693 (paperback) | ISBN 0486806693
Subjects: LCSH: Chaplin, Charlie, 1889–1977—Pictorial works. | Comedy Films—Pictorial works. | BISAC: PERFORMING ARTS / Comedy. | FICTION / General.
Classification: LCC PN2287.C5 T46 2016 | DDC 791.4302/8092—dc23 LC record available at http://lccn.loc.gov/2016007117

Manufactured in the United States by RR Donnelley
80669301 2016
www.doverpublications.com

Contents

Charlie Chaplin as a Man

EVERY now and then there appears on the passing stage of life a personality that recolors individual existence and creates an epoch in the history of the times. Sometimes this force touches the serious problems of life, sometimes it merely entertains. But always it is a vital, living spark that sets ablaze some answering chord in the human breast and sweeps the public off its feet. In lighter vein has come Charlie Chaplin, the most popular comedian in the United States to-day. With pantomime and personality he has captivated the nation.

When the people of this country were frantically searching about for some soothing counterforce against the war depression, public gaze became focused on Chaplin, who immediately sprang into public favor as the greatest entertainer of the time. A glance at the twenty-inch shoes, the little mustache, the limber cane—and the war sinks into oblivion.

A slight-figured little Englishman, disproving for all time the traditional accusation that England lacks humor, trots meekly over the water to America in a vaudeville troupe, is put into motion-picture comedies, and, in one year from that time, carries a million or so people to Laughland and back.

Chaplin's success means more than a mere personal triumph. A new standard of photo-play pantomime has been established. Other screen comedians are racing madly to catch up to his mark—and all of them vainly.

His fun is not ordinarily produced by mere situations, either. The plot, as a rule, is merely a vehicle for the whimsical action of the comedian. His plots are interpreted as they have never been portrayed before. It is not so much what he does as how he does it. You or I could propose to fair Emmaline and not get a smile. Chaplin proposes, and the theater rocks. He reverently kisses the hem of her gown, kneeling at her feet. Utter subjection marks his action.

It is love—hopeless love, for she does not care for him. The theater is sobered. Here is a real drama, even tragedy. Tears come to the eyes, for the whimsical little man is troubled. His lip quivers. Costello could do no better. And then—zip! Behold the comedian again. He sighs, arises, still holding her skirt. The corners of his mouth still droop. He stares with unseeing eyes to the floor. He brings the hem of the skirt again to his face, and carefully, deliberately, and unconcernedly wipes his mouth with it.

The tension breaks. The spectators roar with merriment, and that is real genius. The little man has carried the audience along with him; he has played with their hearts. That is one of the virtues of Chaplin's work—his ability to deepen the comedy and give it contrast.

It is impossible to make a psychological analysis of Chaplin's power. He can tell you of situations, timeliness of action and concentration, but he cannot explain why people laugh.

The world wonders why scientific men probe into the question scientifically and construct a train of theoretical reasons why we laugh. And about that time a new comedy is released which smashes these theories to bits.

Here is something Chaplin has recently stated about his comedy:

"Comedy is a really serious study, but one must not take it seriously. That sounds like a paradox, doesn't it? But it isn't. It is a hard study to learn characters. To make comedy successful there must be an ease, a spontaneity in the action that must not be associated with seriousness. I lay out my plot and study my character thoroughly. I follow him for miles and I go to see him at his work when I know that he doesn't know he is under observation.

"With the plot in my mind, I go before the camera without the slightest notion of what I am going to do. I try to lose myself. I am the character I am representing, and I try to act just as I previously thought that character would act under the same circumstances.

"While the character is working, one has very little time to think. He must act on the spur of the moment. In one hundred feet or less of film there is not time to hesitate. I figure out all of the details beforehand, and thus I get the necessary spontaneity, without which a film looks stilted.

"Naturalness is the greatest requisite of comedy. It must be real and true to life. I believe in realism absolutely. Real things appeal to the people far more quickly than the grotesque. My comedy is actual life, with the slightest twist or exaggeration to bring out what it might be under certain circumstances.

"People want the truth. In the human heart there is a love of truth, and they want this in comedy, too. Spontaneous acting hits the truth nine times out of ten where studied work misses it just as often. There is a time and place for everything. Even in slapstick comedy there is an art. If one hits another at the psychological moment, it is funny. If he does it a moment too early or too late, it misses the mark. And there must be a reason to produce a laugh: To do an unexpected trick, which the audience sees as a logical sequence brings down the house. It is always the little things that bring the laughs."

Chaplin is twenty-five years of age. It wasn't so many years ago that he trotted—barefoot—around the dusty streets of a London suburb, with other children. There are still many of the old citizens of that community who could tell of the slight-figured youngster who climbed out of the oblivion of childhood when he was five years old by appearing on the stage of a London theater.

His parents were both theatrical. Tutored and encouraged by them, he eagerly took up the study, at home, of pantomime, and had become quite a clog dancer when the night of his appearance in a London theater came. The audience literally went wild over him. The second he lifted his feet to the rhythm of the baton and clumped out that first professional dance, the lure of "the boards" was in his heart. That night the seed of his genius was given its first watering. The cheers and applause of the audience, the glare of the footlights, the responsive sound of his feet on the boards, gave birth to the lure.

After that night he went back to school a different boy. His whole dream of the future had been changed. His first appearance on the stage put a resolution in him to return again, and, that time, to stay. He studied in a half-hearted manner, for his whole brain revolved around his career-to-be. He rehearsed in the school yard. All was mimicry. He imitated the schoolteacher, the minister, and the old justice who hobbled by the school every morning. The children forgot their games, to watch him. The teacher, at first provoked and then amused, peered through the window at recess at him. He was intensely in earnest. He turned his acts without the break of a smile.

It was several years later that he received an offer to appear in "Rags and Riches." Originally an American production, this play had been adapted to suit the English fancy. Chaplin took a minor part, and succeeded wonderfully well. He remained until the season closed, and then became possessed of the idea that he wanted to play in heavier parts. He felt that he would be more interested in serious comedy than in the "clownish play," but when he told his parents this, they only laughed at him. He was to be a pantomimist, and nothing else.

Once more he went to school, this time to the Hern Boys' College, near London. After two years more of restless study, he went back to the stage, and this time to remain. Charles Frohman wanted him to play *Billy* with William Gillette in "Sherlock Holmes." In this rôle he was given greater latitude to try his originality, and he succeeded so well that he remained for a long time. His work as *Billy* was not without its serious angles. Comedy was merely intermittent. He liked this.

And then the decisive step into pure pantomime came when he entered vaudeville in London. He says about this:

"It was an accident—my drifting into comedy. Fred Karno was gathering together a bunch of English talent to play 'A Night in an English Music Hall.' This was an altogether new idea in vaudeville. The leading part was supposed to be a drunk—a gentleman drunk—who sits in the box and freely and loudly criticizes the various acts he sees and otherwise takes his own methods of enjoying what he has paid for."

Chaplin took that job, and that night he jumped farther toward the goal of success than he ever had done before. This part was just what his talent needed to develop it. He was a mere boy, and he "put it over." He worked hard to perfect himself in the part, and searched all of London for drunks. When he found odd types, he followed and studied them for hours, absorbing the characteristics of a whisky-soaked brain and body.

This same practice of seeking the truth in perfecting his parts is still a mania with Chaplin. To-day, in film work, he spends the greater part of his time studying types of the characters he is to portray. This is a conscientious search for realism.

After playing in England for a long time, the company decided to go to America. Over this, Chaplin rejoiced. He had always desired to go to America, and now he could go with a future all laid out for him.

The United States liked both "A Night in an English Music Hall" and Chaplin. Americans liked him so well that he was snapped up by film producers in no time. He wouldn't give in at first, for he had never thought of acting for the camera, and wanted to deliberate over it. Finally he consented, and appeared in his first picture.

The studio lights certainly fertilized Chaplin's budding genius. His ability produced unprecedented pantomime and spontaneity. Gradually he deepened his work, and, as he thus bared his new action and funny little movements, the public became wildly understanding and enthusiastic.

"Chaplinitis" impended.

Motion-picture fans spread the good word of a new personality in comedy. Here was an entirely different sort of comedy. This man was different. Boys and girls would go home and tell their parents how good the show was. "Well, how do you mean he was funny?" the mothers asked. They couldn't explain. They laughed, and that was the only reason they could give.

Chaplin soon had the weather outrivaled as a conversation topic. The boys and girls sauntering home from school tried to imitate his walk. Out of this grew song and dance. Women at the clubs discussed him. Business men over their lunches laughed at some recollection of his latest stunt. The newspapers began writing about him. Magazines clamored for his pictures. Caricatures were made of him for the newspapers, and serious-minded business men at the office tried to mimic him. School children hurried from their studies in a frenzy of eagerness to get to the nearest Chaplin theater. The billboards and fences were covered with posters.

The country was Chaplin mad!

Every one talked Chaplin. Picture-show exhibitors fought for rights to his films. In every town and hamlet and in every corner of every large city "Chaplin To-night" signs were hung out.

Among the children, both of the rich sections and of the slums, an imitation of Chaplin is considered humorous. To be "Chaplinesque" is to be witty. To crunch about in a pair of run-over shoes and squint an eye is the proper form of entertainment in élite circles. One who can recite at a dinner table the description of the latest Chaplin picture and recite it so Chaplin is visualized, is a good entertainer.

To be able to produce something which will make the masses laugh—that is real achievement. Chaplin sends his humor out in two-thousand-foot lots through the country the only way in which one man can simultaneously bring joy to millions.

The first Essanay-Chaplin comedy, "His New Job," shall always be a classic in the mind of Essanay employees. Chaplin stood out on the center of the floor and executed a clog dance. He danced for about five minutes while the other players gazed at him—puzzled. Some laughed. Others frowned. Then he woke up and chuckled.

"All right, boys," he shouted; "shoot your set! I'm all ready. A little pep all around—a little pep, please!"

Chaplin then went through a few other queer steps, and then stood to one side and sized up the situation. He examined the set and the actors. He instructed them in the sense of the first scene—in a rapid-fire voice to which all nervously and tensely listened.

Chaplin is hard to work with, because he is not easily understood. He thinks faster than others. But, then, he is appreciative, and praises audibly when praise is justified. Chaplin always has a superb cast because he rapidly eliminates poor support.

He is a worker. "Pantomime is one per cent inspiration and ninety-nine per cent perspiration" with Chaplin, adapting the late Elbert Hubbard's definition of genius. He is on the floor all day, with his coat off between scenes, and even helping to move the scenery about. Chaplin is very earnest in his work. He seldom smiles. He demands in a soft voice, but there is cold steel behind it.

"Comedy is a funny thing," said Chaplin. "It is a thing which has developed up to a certain point, retrograded, and come back to that point again. It has never progressed beyond that point. We think it has developed all through the ages. We get this illusion of development from its fluctuations, its characteristics as it has been preferred by the various generations and nationalities. The comedy that amuses the world to-day is identical with that which brought laughter to the Babylonians, the Greeks, and the Romans. Every age of history is eaten up by the egotism of men. Every age thinks that the world has reached the highest point of the development in itself. That is because the man of this age sees himself as the center of the picture.

"I have a theory that comedy increases in refinement in inverse proportion to the refinement of the world in which it appears. I mean that the more intellectual the world is, the more boisterous will be the successful comedy of that world.

"A barbarian has very little sense of humor. What he has is very delicate. Horseplay would not be successful with him. He wants something that is a little out of the ordinary. The poor misshapen jester of the Middle Ages was a most indifferent comedian, according to our idea of humor. He played on words and mimicked a courtier, or a general, or a woman who happened to be out of favor at court. His witty sayings were puns. He voiced great truths while in an attitude that his hearers fondly believed was funny, and he passed as a humorist. He was the end man in the world's minstrel show. His interlocutor was a condescending baron or king. Then, hitting a man on the head with a mallet was not funny. That was everyday stuff, and the jester used it only when his originality gave out. The situation at that time was nothing. The epigram was the thing, did one desire to cause a laugh."

The human side of Chaplin is never evident. The friends about him are subjected to his personality, and, thus feeling this mysterious absence of personal ego, stare and wonder. Has he ever had a love affair? Is he sentimental? What sort of books does he read? Is he Socialist—or what?

Such questions arise as one gazes at the little Englishman, and yet we'll never see the bottom of his heart. When we ask, he says:

"What difference does it make whether I eat mustard with ice cream or put sugar in beer, except on the screen?"

This collection of narratives is the fiction version of Charlie Chaplin's best pictures, and has been written with the view of giving the reader something unusual, still maintaining all the humor of the films.

On the following pages, ten of these photo plays which gained for Charlie Chaplin the reputation he is enjoying as being the funniest of funny men, are offered in the form of ten separate and complete short stories, with all the life, comedy, and action of the pictures on which they are based.

The Bank

CHARLIE CHAPLIN came walking briskly along the street. There was something different about his appearance. His shabby shoes, baggy trousers, and well-worn derby were the same. Likewise, his frayed necktie "rode" his collar fore and aft as usual, and his little, closely buttoned coat had not been replaced by a new and better-fitting garment. In point of costume, there was no change whatever in his outward aspect.

But this was a different Charlie, none the less. You could see that at a glance. Walking on his heels, with his toes turned out at right angles, his feet came down on the pavement with a new precision, for all that they still appeared to be suffering from an aggravated case of corns, spring halt, spavin—all the ailments to which the pedal extremities of man or animal are heir.

His little bamboo cane he no longer twirled as he waddled along. Now he held that swagger stick stiffly through the middle, as a marshal of France in the days of Napoleon might have carried his baton, and no less proudly. His head, with its crop of bushy hair, and his battered derby perched on top of that, he held erect. His narrow shoulders were squared importantly—*that,* in a word, was the explanation of the difference in him. His whole bearing radiated an air of importance.

What was it that had lent this surprising dignity to his carriage?

Charlie continued his proud, his almost haughty, progress along the street. That fall which proverbially follows upon the heels of pride almost overtook him. He stumbled over an infinitesimal something on the sidewalk. And yet he did not rail at the inanimate object that had menaced his equilibrium. Retracing his steps to it, he flattened it out with a tap of the sole of his shoe. And then he resumed his lofty way up the street.

In at the imposing white marble front of an office building Charlie turned. The massive columns at either side of that entrance bore, on tablets of bronze, the terse information that herein was to be found the Two Hundred and Ninety-second National Bank.

Charlie crossed the ground floor of the office building, with his eyes fixed on a point in the air before him from which he disdained to remove them to recognize the existence of the cigar-stand proprietor, the elevator man or starter, and passed through the two glass entrance doors of the bank that stood open at the rear of the lobby.

The tellers and bookkeepers who were getting their cash and ledgers in order in the cages in preparation for the day's business—these Charlie ignored utterly and completely, as persons beneath his notice, also, as he moved toward the president's office.

Boldly throwing open the door of that sacred precinct, Charlie passed through it and into the room beyond. Here, from nine to five each day, Miss Edna Lovely, the president's private stenographer, toiled at her typewriter. It was only eight-forty-five now. She had not yet arrived to take up her daily duties. Charlie crossed the room and opened the door that gave into a narrow hall outside, and along this hall he strode—still with that air of importance—to the head of a flight of marble stairs that led into the basement of the bank.

Descending the stairs, one at a time, Charlie advanced upon the great steel door of the bank's vault that was set into the solid concrete of the basement's wall.

He twirled the dial of the combination once to the right, twice to the left. Then he looked off into space from under a frown of concentration, while his lips moved as though he was repeating a series of numbers. With a satisfied nod, he returned his attention to the dial, and twirled it rapidly round. A brief pause to consult a number written on his cuff. Then another satisfied nod, and again he twirled the dial. Seizing the wheel which operated the bolts of the vault door, he turned it slowly and the vault door swung open.

Charlie stepped into the safe, to emerge from it in a moment with a pail and a mop.

From the pail he removed a long blue coat with brass buttons down the front, and a white duck cap with a patent-leather peak. He put on the cap and the coat, and he was arrayed in the uniform of his office and ready for the day's work. And incidentally the explanation of the air of importance which he had shown in his bearing all along was now disclosed.

Charlie Chaplin was the janitor of that bank.

Waddling over to the water faucet at the other end of the basement, Charlie half filled his pail. Then, dropping the mop in it, he lifted the bucket and started back upstairs.

Beside the desk in the foyer of the bank that was presided over by a young man who took the visitors' cards, sat a powerfully built man with a black mustache who held a roll of paper in his hand that resembled the diploma of a college graduate in size.

Between the young man at the visitors' desk and this caller Charlie halted.

He removed the dripping mop from the pail and absent-mindedly stuck it up in the visitor's high hat, which he had placed on the floor beside the chair in which he sat.

"Look what you're doing!" sharply admonished the young man at the desk.

Charlie, turning to follow the direction of the young man's pointing finger, saw the handle of the mop sticking up out of the stranger's hat, and he smiled at the burly caller apologetically, and tipped his cap at him. The latter, inarticulate with rage, watched Charlie remove the mop from his hat. And then he picked it up from the floor and clapped it on his head.

Enough water from the mop to half fill it had remained in the hat after Charlie had withdrawn the swab of rags on the end of the pole from the repository where he had accidentally placed it, and the broad-shouldered stranger's head, face, and collar were deluged.

He bounded up.

"You——" he spluttered angrily.

Charlie, who had picked up his pail, and was starting off with the mop over his shoulder, turned as he heard the visitor address him.

And the mop smacked wetly full in the face of the young man at the desk.

"Can't you be careful?" expostulated the latter.

"You bungling blockhead!" bellowed the brawny caller.

Charlie, with the mop still over his shoulder, turned to apologize to the young man whose face he had swiped with it. In doing so, he knocked the stranger's hat off.

"I'll have you fired for this!" roared the latter.

Charlie turned back to him. The mop again gave the face of the young man at the desk an unasked-for wash. Charlie tipped his cap to the tall, thickset caller once more.

"Beg pardon—I'm going right away!"

And, turning to suit the action to the words, he slapped him in the face with the mop, sending him tumbling backward into the chair from which he had risen, and waddled off.

Before the closed door of the president's office, Charlie halted. From within came the sound of sweeping, which indicated to Charlie that his assistant, Mike, was at work. Charlie heard the sweeping suddenly stop. There was absolute silence from the room on the other side of the door.

"Loafing, eh?" Charlie murmured to himself, while his brows drew together in a reproving frown. "I'll have to put a stop to that!"

He opened the door and strode in upon his assistant.

With a can of coffee steaming before him on the president's desk, the assistant was eating a sandwich from a paper bag. The sandwich seemingly had been made of a whole loaf of bread, split in half, and with a piece of meat of the length, width, and breadth of a porterhouse steak inserted between it.

A third of the sandwich was in the assistant's mouth. Despite the fact that he could not in reason expect it to hold any more, he was nevertheless in the act of trying to transfer another third of the sandwich in his hand to his mouth as Charlie entered the room.

"What are you doing?" Charlie demanded.

The assistant made a series of inarticulate sounds through the bread and meat with which his mouth was stuffed.

"What's that?"

The assistant mumbled again.

Charlie advanced to the desk and picked up the president's penholder. With the end of it he freed the assistant's mouth of its impediment of speech.

"Now, what did you say?" he inquired.

"I said I was eatin'," replied the assistant.

Charlie turned away and lifted his mop from the pail.

"Work!" he ordered succinctly. As he spoke, his eye roved critically over the room in search of a nook or corner that the other might have left undusted, and which would entitle him to a further rebuke, while at the same time he wrung out the mop unwittingly over the can of coffee on the desk.

Then, discovering the can there for the first time, and also that his assistant's back was turned, Charlie picked up the tin receptacle and took a pull at it.

He blew the coffee out again hurriedly—it tasted too much of mop to suit even his unfastidious taste.

"Can't I even take a drink of me coffee first?" asked his assistant, in a complaining tone.

Charlie looked from him to the can, which he had hastily set down on the desk again after sampling its contents. Then, with a shrug, he waved his hand leniently toward it.

"All right," he assented. "Take a good, long drink, too—it may make you work better."

His assistant raised the can to his lips. He followed Charlie's advice about taking a good drink—he drained the can to the bottom. Then, setting it down, he smacked his lips with evident relish. Charlie, who had been watching him, turned pale. He clapped his hand over his mouth and passed through the room into that of the president's private stenographer.

Picking up a broom, he began to sweep up the paper with which the floor was littered. When he had it swept up into a pile, he sent it scattering through the open door into the president's office, where his assistant was wielding his own broom once more on the paper scattered over the floor there.

The assistant, who thought he had swept up all the paper in that office, turned around, and his eyes bulged as he looked at the vast heap of it behind him which Charlie had put there.

It took the assistant only a moment or two to perceive how the paper had got into the office which he had just swept clean. A moment more, and he was sweeping it back through the door into the stenographer's office, where Charlie, believing his work through, was about to depart.

It was Charlie's turn, on looking around at the floor behind him, to gaze bewilderedly at the mass of paper which, it seemed, had sprung up by magic on the carpet over which he had just wielded the broom.

Then he, too, realized how the stuff had got there.

"Mike!" he called.

His assistant appeared in the doorway of the president's office. Charlie, pointing to the paper that the other had swept back into the stenographer's room from which it had come, turned to leave with his mop and pail.

"You put it there," he said briefly. "Now you clean it up yourself."

Meanwhile, the burly visitor who had been waiting in the foyer of the bank for the president to arrive, bounded suddenly up out of his chair and began to unroll the paper that looked like a diploma in his hands.

The president had just come into the bank.

"I want to sell you these bonds, sir!" the powerfully built stranger announced.

"Not interested!" snapped the president.

He tried to pass by the visitor. The latter waved the document under his nose.

"I've got to sell these bonds to you," he insisted, "or I am a ruined man. Buy them, sir! Oh, buy them, I beg of you! You had a mother once, didn't you? No—that's got nothing to do with this case! What I meant to say was, think of your own wife and little children——"

The president succeeded in dodging around the importunate visitor and hastened off toward the door of his private office.

"Not interested! Not interested!" he snapped back over his shoulder.

The big man stood looking blankly after him for a moment. Then, his jaw closing determinedly, he rolled up the document which he carried with him and sat down beside the young man at the visitors' desk again.

"I'll wait," he grimly informed the latter. "He's got to buy these bonds—and, perhaps, he'll be willing to listen to me a little later. I want you to take my card in to him, at fifteen-minute intervals, all day long."

"I don't think Mr. Gridley will see you, sir," the young man prophesied. "He said he wasn't interested in buying any bonds from you to-day. And what he says is usually final."

The burly man settled himself more firmly in his chair.

"I'll wait," he repeated, his lips tightening purposefully. "If he won't see me in his office, he'll be passing by here some time during the day, and I'll get a chance to put my case up to him then."

Charlie, descending the steps to the basement of the bank with his mop and pail, had come upon his assistant, who, with a bucket beside him, was washing down those same stairs.

"You thought you was smart, didn't you," Mike addressed him, "leavin' all that paper for me to clean up out o' both them offices, when it was your job to sweep out one, anyway?"

Charlie continued his descent of the stairs without deigning to reply.

"I'm gettin' tired o' doin' all the work around here while you take it easy, I'll tell you that," his assistant went on, mounting ire in his tone. "I'll tell you that!"

Charlie, stiffly silent, stepped down at the end of the staircase, and one foot went into his assistant's bucket. He clumped away with it still on his foot. Mike, reaching for the pail a moment later, found it gone. He jumped up and hurled the rag with which he had been washing the stairs to the floor.

"Another one of his tricks!" he raged. "He won't do his own work, and he won't leave me to do mine! But this is right where I have a show-down with that young feller! Yes, sir, right now!"

Mike turned to go after Charlie. He found the latter, who had freed his foot of his assistant's pail and set down his own bucket and the mop in a corner of the basement, and was on his way back upstairs into the bank, standing behind him.

Mike walked up to him and thrust his face into his.

"I can lick you!" Charlie's assistant informed him.

Charlie frowned sternly at him.

"You forget yourself," he announced coldly. "I have told you, a dozen times before, that when you speak to me you must say 'sir.' "

Mike ground his teeth.

"I'm goin' to punch your head off, sir!" he grated between them. "Do you like that any better, sir? Then, how do you like—this?"

With the last word, he launched a blow at Charlie's head. Charlie ducked, and came up unscathed. He side-stepped and danced before his assistant on his toes, with his fists revolving around each other.

"I'll have to teach you your place, it seems," said he. "Here—hold my hat!"

He held out his cap to Mike, who took it.

"Hold my coat!" Charlie ordered him, removing it as he spoke.

Mike took that, also. And then Charlie hit him a wallop that sent him four feet through the air, to sprawl on all fours on the floor.

"Now, bring me my cap," Charlie ordered.

His assistant obediently did so.

"Hold my coat!" Charlie next ordered him.

Mike obeyed, and Charlie put his arms in it and buttoned it around him again. Then, without so much as a glance behind him at his vanquished assistant, he marched away up the stairs toward the main floor of the bank, for which he had been bound before Mike had sought to "lick" him—with such disastrous consequences to himself.

Charlie passed by the calendar on the wall of the bank, above the marble ledges that were for the customers' convenience in signing checks or making out their deposit slips, all unconscious of the importance of the date, "May 26th," which was blazoned forth in foot-high black letters there.

The date marked an event in the life of Charles Careful, the cashier of the bank. It was his birthday.

Though Charlie Chaplin was unaware of this fact, there was another employee of the Ninety-second National who was not. That other was Miss Edna Lovely, the president's private stenographer.

The cashier of the bank was not over thirty-five. He had been called handsome by other people than his mother. And, in addition, he was what is known as a "good dresser." Miss Edna had long ago confessed to herself that she was in love with him. She believed that the cashier was not wholly indifferent to her own attractions. But, the bashfulest of bashful men, he had not yet mustered up sufficient courage to ask her if his affection was returned.

Here, she had decided, was a chance to let him know that his love was by no means in vain. For his birthday, she had bought him a pretty necktie in a box. And now she inserted a piece of paper in her machine, and on it wrote:

"To Charlie, *with love,*
"from Edna."

She removed the sheet from the typewriter and read those two lines upon it, with a smile. *That* would embolden him to speak, surely. It would show him that he had nothing to fear in laying his heart at her feet, since she had thus confessed her own love for him.

Rising, the girl left the box with the necktie in it and the sheet of paper with its two lines of typewriting beside it lying on the desk, while she went to find a sheet of paper large enough to wrap up the gift for its presentation to the cashier.

Charlie Chaplin wandered into her room not a moment after she had vacated it.

Now, Charlie—a sentimentalist ever—had not worked for that bank a day before he had given his heart unreservedly to the president's fair stenographer. Though he loved her in silence, it was none the less ardently.

She might spurn his offer of matrimony on a janitor's salary, if he were to make it to her. She might even complain to the president, and ask that he be discharged, if he spoke to her of love. And that was what had restrained Charlie from mentioning the state of his feelings toward her—he had been afraid that it would cost him his job.

Now, however, his eye fell on the necktie in the box on her desk. He picked it up and looked it over.

"It's a nice tie," he murmured.

And then, as he put the box down where he had found it, his glance dropped on the note beside it. Lifting that, too, he slowly spelled out the words:

"To Charlie, w*ith love,*
"from Edna."

A joyous expression overspread Charlie's face. She had meant the necktie for *him!* It was a present, a little token of the place he occupied in her regard. *With love.* So she had guessed his secret all along. And—this had been meant to let him know that his love for her was reciprocated. She cared for him, too!

The door opened, and the girl came back into the room.

Charlie, stepping from her desk to the stand on which rested the letter press, giggled embarrassedly. With one finger in his mouth, he shrugged his shoulders from side to side. The girl, seating herself at her desk, looked around at him over her shoulder.

"How do you do?" said Charlie, tipping his cap to her.

She began to wrap up the necktie and the note in the box.

"Hello, Charlie!" she greeted him indifferently.

Charlie Chaplin pulled his frayed necktie up over the top of his long, brass-buttoned coat, and fingered it smilingly.

"Ahem!" he coughed softly.

The girl looked around at him again.

"This one's getting pretty well worn out, isn't it?" Charlie asked her, glancing down at his necktie in his fingers.

"It's a disgrace," she answered shortly.

Then she turned back once more and went on wrapping up the box. Charlie giggled again. He spun the wheel of the letter press round with one hand. Instantly an expression of anguish settled on his face. He had screwed his other hand into the press. He spun the wheel around again, releasing his imprisoned fingers, and laughed self-consciously once more as he found the girl's eyes upon him. He made a quick gesture toward the box she had partially wrapped up by this time.

"Somebody's going to get a present, aren't they?" he asked.

"They are," she agreed.

Charlie opened the door. He hesitated on the threshold, and then he blurted:

"I know who it's for!" and he threw her a kiss. "Oh, *you!*"

And the next moment he was gone.

In the president's office, which was temporarily deserted, Charlie stood looking at the door behind which sat the fair being for whose sake he felt that dying would be but a blissful privilege. He threw another kiss at that closed door. Then, lifting his arms from his sides, he let them fall again—the gesture of the hero in the melodrama when he takes leave of the heroine to ride forth upon a mission of danger for His Majesty, the King.

Turning on his heel, Charlie walked—bouncing his shoulders up and down—to the other door. He turned once more and threw another kiss at the panels of the door behind which the stenographer sat, repeating the gesture with his arms. Then he flung open the door, and turned simultaneously to dash out of it—with the result that his head collided with its panels, and he sprawled on the floor.

Picking himself up, Charlie approached the door stiffly. He raised his cap to it. And then he walked through it on his heels.

Just as Charlie was crossing the foyer of the bank, he saw the black-mustached man of powerful build, who had been waiting to see the president again to endeavor to persuade him to change his mind about buying his bonds, spring up once more and begin to unroll the document in his hands as the president approached on the way to his private office from a trip he had made to the paying teller's cage.

"You must listen to me, sir," the stalwart visitor exclaimed, "while I tell you of the value of these bonds. Buy them, and you will secure the bargain of a lifetime. I will sell them to you for——"

The president stopped angrily before him.

"You will *not* sell me your bonds," he announced, "for any amount. I wouldn't buy them from you for a ten-cent piece. I wouldn't even take them from you as a gift. Is that perfectly clear? Then allow me to bid you good day!"

The burly caller seemed to swell to twice his size with wrath. He rolled up the document which he carried, and turned on his heel.

"You will pay for this!" he called back over his shoulder, as he strode toward the gate in the railing which separated the waiting room in the foyer of the bank from the open space outside, where the depositors and other customers of the institution could line up at the windows of the various cages. "You will pay—mark my words!"

Charlie, looking after the man in surprise at the excessive rage which filled him, was aroused by the president's voice beside him.

"Here, you," said the president, holding out a legal-size letter to him; "mail this."

Charlie took the letter, and tipped his cap.

"Yes, sir!" he said, and he waddled in the big man's wake toward the letter chute.

The husky visitor was leaning against one of those marble ledges against the wall of the bank, tugging at his black mustache, while his massive chest rose and fell volcanically with the rage that still surged within it.

Charlie halted before him, and looked up into his face. He pressed his hand to his cheek, and shook his head in sorrowing surprise.

Then, taking the man's unresisting hand in his, he felt of his pulse.

"Oh, dear me!" Charlie exclaimed under his breath.

He addressed the other:

"Will you put out your tongue, and let me see it?"

The man accommodated him. Charlie took a stamp from his pocket, and, applying it to the surface of the extended tongue, he transferred it to the envelope which the president of the bank had given him.

"Thank you," he nodded to the disappointed bond seller.

And, tipping his cap to him, without another word he waddled away to the mail chute.

Charlie tried to put the letter in widthwise. It didn't fit the slot that way, of course. He tried again, and a third time. Then, tearing the letter in three pieces, he stuffed one after the other down the chute. After which, turning around on his heels, he waddled back the way he had come—serene in the knowledge that he had carried out the errand on which the president had sent him.

Five minutes later, holding in one hand a ten-cent bunch of flowers—comprising three wilted and "wired" roses, which he had purchased from an Italian vender on the sidewalk outside the bank—Charlie Chaplin was laboriously pushing a pen in the other across a scrap of paper.

He held the scrap of paper up, and read the result of his literary efforts:

"To Edna, *with love,*
"from Charlie."

With a sigh of satisfaction, Charlie rose, with the bunch of flowers and the note, and retraced his steps to the stenographer's room. She had again stepped out of it for a moment, Charlie perceived through the crack in the door, which he cautiously opened. Though he did not know it, she was at that moment presenting the cashier with the necktie she had bought him for his birthday.

Charlie laid the flowers down on her desk, with the note beside them. He kissed the tip of his finger, and applied it in turn to each one of the already-withering roses, and also to the keys of her open typewriter. Then he stole out of the room again.

Miss Edna, returning, saw the flowers and the note on the desk. They were from the cashier, she supposed—as was natural, since it was his Christian name that was signed to the scrap of paper, as well as Charlie Chaplin's.

Raising the flowers to her lips, she was just imprinting a kiss upon them when the cashier himself entered—to show her how well the necktie, which he had put on, became him.

"Thank you for these!" the girl told the cashier.

He stared from her to the flowers, which she was holding against her cheek.

"Those?" he repeated blankly. "Why—I didn't give them to you! There must be some mistake!"

"Didn't you write this note?" she demanded, handing him the scrap of paper on which Charlie had confessed to her in writing that he was her willing slave.

The cashier laughed heartily.

"Of course I didn't!" said he. "That's Charlie, the janitor—I recognize his handwriting, or his apology for it, rather. That's a good joke on you!"

And, still laughing, he departed.

The door of the president's office opened a crack. Charlie Chaplin looked in upon the stenographer, who held his bunch of flowers in one hand, his note in the other. She had got them, all right! But slowly the joyous light faded out of his face. He watched Miss Edna hurl the cheap bouquet into the wastebasket. Then he saw her tear the note in half, drop it to the floor, and set her foot indignantly upon it.

"Fool!" he heard her say.

And then she swept from the room. Charlie crept into it after she had gone and recovered his flowers from the wastebasket. He stuffed them out of sight under his coat, and crept out of the office again.

On his way down into the basement of the bank, Charlie came face to face with the cashier.

Charlie stopped and stared at the necktie which the latter was wearing. It was the identical one he had seen in the box on the stenographer's desk. Charlie took off his cap and scratched his head in perplexity. But the note he had seen beside the box had said plainly enough: "To Charlie, with love."

How, then, had the thing got around this man's neck? Charlie lifted the end of the necktie, as he stood before the cashier, and felt of it. It *was* the same one! Charlie gave up the riddle as too much for him to solve. The necktie must have been meant for him, but, nevertheless, the cashier now had it. Charlie let the end of the necktie fall from his fingers, with a contemptuous sniff.

"I don't think much of it, anyway!" he announced.

He turned to continue his way to the basement, but halted before he had taken two steps. As he had looked about he was confronted by two girls, who, so Charlie thought, were just what a girl should be. Leaning unconsciously against a woman who was engaged at the cashier's window, Charlie coughed his old reliable cough on which he always depended to attract attention of one to whom he was too bashful to speak. Then, as he saw them turn, Charlie's face lit up with a smile. They smiled back. Charlie was about to venture a word when he was startled by a door slamming, and, looking past the girls, he saw the president come out of his office. His smile vanished quickly, and without a word he spun around on his heel and walked swiftly down to the basement, abandoning flirting.

"Business before pleasure," he murmured to himself, as he reached the foot of the stairs, seeking to console himself.

In the basement he seated himself on a bench against the wall beside which leaned his mop. From under his coat he drew out the despised bunch of flowers. He turned the thing over in his hand hesitatingly. An ash can stood at his elbow. He lifted the cover, and was about to consign the bouquet to it—but he changed his mind.

Stuffing the nosegay under his coat again, he leaned back on the bench. The minutes passed. All was very still. Charlie's chin nodded down on his breast.

It seemed to him that suddenly the silence of the bank was shattered by no less than six shots fired in rapid succession from a revolver.

Charlie sat bolt upright on the bench.

What had happened? he asked himself.

The answer to that question was this: The burly, black-mustached man who had tried in vain to dispose of his bonds to the president of the bank, had attempted to make good his threat that the latter would pay for having refused to yield to his request.

Leaving the bank, he had repaired to a low dive frequented by denizens of the underworld, and there he had enlisted the services of four desperate characters.

They had entered the bank after three o'clock, when the president, his stenographer, and the cashier were in the chief executive's private office, counting up the day's cash which lay in bags of gold and stacks of bills on the president's desk.

The black-mustached would-be seller of the bonds had gone down in the basement with two of his accomplices, while the two other crooks had made their way toward the room where the president, his stenographer, and the cashier sat.

With three bags of gold, the cashier had just left the president's office with the stenographer for the vault in the basement.

And then the two crooks had burst in upon the president, as he sat alone before his desk, and opened fire on him with their revolvers. It was these shots that Charlie had heard. But now, as he sat up straight on the bench in the basement, he heard something else. It was a woman's cry for help, and near at hand.

Charlie bounded up, and ran in the direction of the cry.

The two crooks who had gone into the basement with the black-mustached leader of the gang had grappled with the cashier and the stenographer upon their arrival there with the three bags of gold. The cashier had struggled loose and run back upstairs. But Miss Edna had been lifted off her feet, despite her struggles, and was being borne toward the vault—when Charlie Chaplin dashed upon the scene.

He slapped one of the crooks on the wrist, which made him drop his gun.

Then, with a well-placed kick in the stomach, he sent him sailing backward through the air and into the vault through its open door.

He served the second of the two crooks with a kick the same way.

Then, turning his attention to the leader of the gang, he leaped on his chest, and, seizing his high hat by the brim, pulled it down over his eyes and nose and mouth. Then, turning him around, he forced him to adopt the posture of a man stooping over to pick up a dollar bill on the sidewalk. And, with another kick, he sent him, too, sprawling into the vault.

Charlie grasped the door and swung it shut. He twirled the dial of the combination—and three of the five rascals were out of harm's way.

Then Charlie turned his attention to the stenographer, who had collapsed in a dead faint on the floor.

Picking her up in his arms, Charlie slung her over his shoulder. He stooped and secured the gun which his slap on the wrist had caused the first of the crooks he had tackled to drop. And then, with his fair burden hanging half down his back, and the weapon gripped firmly in one hand, Charlie ran upstairs to round up the rest of the gang.

And that was what he did, alone and single-handed. Later, after the police had come and gone with their prisoners, and Charlie stood beside the stenographer in the president's office, receiving his congratulations, a head was thrust out from under the president's desk—it was the cashier, who had run up from the basement and hid there, like a coward.

"You are no longer the cashier of this bank," the president sternly told him. "I shall henceforth intrust that position to a braver man than you—Charlie Chaplin!"

Nor was that all Charlie had won by his heroism.

"Have you still got those roses you gave me?" Miss Edna asked softly, following him into her room and running her arm through his.

Charlie pulled the faded little bouquet from under his coat and gave them to her. He turned, after a moment, to meet her eyes over the withered flowers—which she was pressing to her lips.

"Then you *do* love me?" Charlie asked her eagerly.

She nodded. And he took her into his arms. He stroked her hair, kissing it. It surprised him to find out what coarse hair she really had. It had always looked as fine as spun gold to him. But, stroking it under his fingers for the first time, he found that it was tough as the rags of a mop!

Charlie woke up. It *was* the mop beside the bench on which he was sitting that he had been stroking and kissing instead of the stenographer's head. He stared, bewildered, around him. Then, rising, he hastened off upstairs.

The first persons he met were Miss Edna and the cashier.

"Hasn't the bank been robbed?" Charlie asked him.

"Not that I know of," replied the cashier, with a start of surprise.

Charlie rubbed his hand over his forehead.

"You're sure the bank hasn't lost anything?" he insisted.

The cashier placed his arm around the stenographer's waist and started to lead her away with him. Charlie thought he heard him whisper something to the girl about "drinking," and "that's the trouble with most janitors." The cashier answered his question over his shoulder sharply, as he was moving off with her:

"No, the bank hasn't lost anything."

Charlie stood looking after them. So it had all been only a dream! He drew the bunch of wilted flowers from under his coat, looking from them to the departing cashier and the girl. At that moment, Charlie saw the cashier stoop and kiss her. With a shrug, he tossed the bouquet into the air and kicked it aside when it came down with a quick flirt of his foot behind him.

"Well, the bank's *going* to lose something," announced Charlie in an undertone. "And that's me as its janitor!"

A Woman

ON a bench in the park three people were sitting, a man, a woman, and a young and beautiful girl.

They were husband, wife, and daughter. On one side of the man, his wife slept. On the other, his daughter also slumbered. The man's head swayed drowsily; his chin bobbed down in his breast; he was just about to join them in the land of dreams. And then suddenly he became wide awake.

Along the park walk, a young lady came strolling. She was fashionably—another woman might have said flashily—dressed. Also, she was pretty. Not more so than the man's daughter. But then she was not his daughter. And that made all the difference.

The man sat up straight on the bench and brushed the ends of his bushy mustache with a flourish. As the young lady passed, taking advantage of the fact that his wife and daughter on either side of him were asleep, he lowered one eyelid and raised it again.

The girl turned around and winked back.

The man slid forward to the edge of the bench. He looked down at his wife. Her eyes were closed, without a flicker of the lids, and even as he glanced at her a faint but unmistakable snore floated from between her slightly parted lips. He looked at his daughter next. She, too, was still sound asleep. Rising cautiously from the bench between them, he stole away from the seat on his tiptoes—after the girl who had answered his wink in kind.

"Good morning!" the man greeted her around a bend in the walk, lifting his high hat, with a bow.

The girl stopped before a bench that happened to be standing vacant there, and looked up at him, with a smile that registered no hint of displeasure at his daring, a stranger, to address her.

"Oh, why, how do you do?" she exclaimed in the tone of one who is surprised, and at the same time pleased, at unexpectedly meeting an old friend.

She seated herself on the bench, with an inviting lift of her eyebrows. The man promptly sat down beside her. And, with the same alacrity, he encircled her waist with his arm.

"What is there about me that makes you like me so much?" he inquired confidentially.

"You're so handsome!" she replied.

The man brushed up the ends of his mustache under a nose that made up in quantity for what it lacked in quality of symmetry and other details of beauty, and raised a pair of cross eyes of a pea-green hue to the neighboring trees, with a self-satisfied smile that seemed to say to those inanimate observers of his tête-à-tête with the girl: "You see what a perfect rascal I am with the ladies, when I want to be!"

At that moment, across the sward back of the bench on which they sat, a young man came walking, in defiance of the signs which were stuck up in the turf with their warning, "Keep Off the Grass."

He was short of stature and slight of build.

On his upper lip was a little black mustache, which shifted from side to side as he set down first one foot and then the other in a manner reminiscent of the German militia's "goose step."

Perched squarely on top of his bushy hair was a derby of at least ten summers, that looked as though it felt every winter of it. His coat was short, rusty with age, and buttoned tight across his insignificant chest. His trousers were baggy enough to suit the sartorial fancy of even a Hollander. In his hand he carried a little bamboo cane, which he twirled blithely as he shoved himself along, rather than walked, on the heels of a pair of dilapidated shoes that any self-respecting rubbish heap would have picked itself up and moved away rather than have submitted to the insult of receiving.

A tramp of the comic-weekly type was what the young man looked like. And yet he seemed happy, without a care in the world. That is, until he caught sight of the man and the girl on the bench ahead of him. At once his expression became woebegone, and he ceased the blithe twirling of his cane.

That was how the sight of lovers spooning together on a bench always affected our hero, who—as you will doubtless have guessed before this—was none other than Charlie Chaplin.

It saddened him to think that another had a pretty girl to spoon with while he had not, and made him want to set out at once to rectify that mistake. Any pretty girl at such a time would do—even the one the other fellow happened to be spooning with. Now Charlie approached the bench on which the cross-eyed man with the bushy mustache was sitting with the girl, and stopped beside her.

He attracted her attention to his presence by hooking the handle of his cane around her arm and giving it a couple of gentle pulls.

When she looked around at him, Charlie raised his battered derby to her, with a smile.

"Don't you want to take a little walk with me?" he inquired softly.

The man who had left his wife and daughter asleep on the other bench around the bend in the path arose and confronted Charlie threateningly.

"You take a little walk all by yourself," he ordered sternly—"quick, too!"

Charlie, instead of obeying, sat down on the end of the bench beside the girl.

"It's funny," he informed her, "that I've never seen you in the park before as long as I've been stopping here!"

The girl tittered.

"Say, I'm talking to you!" the cross-eyed man addressed him again. "Do you know it?"

Charlie surveyed him without rising.

"You're looking at me, too, I suppose," said he, "but I wouldn't know that."

This time the girl's laugh rang out unrestrained. And the man's bushy mustache fairly bristled with anger, as he glared at Charlie—or, rather, tried to; for, due to the hopeless manner in which his eyes were crossed, it was his own nose that received the benefit of that baleful glower.

"I tell you," he fumed at Charlie, "to move on!"

Charlie rose. He knocked the man's hat off with his little cane, and then sat down again.

"Always take your hat off," Charlie admonished him, his own still resting on top of his crop of bushy hair, "in the presence of a lady."

The man opened his mouth three separate times to speak, before the wrath that had boiled up in him would permit him to do so. Then, shaking his fist under Charlie's nose.

"I'll go and get a cop!" he announced. "He'll run you in for what you are—a tramp! If I had anything to do with it, you'd stay in jail for the rest of your life after you landed there, too! But just wait here!"

And he hurried off to find a policeman into whose custody he could place Charlie, on the charge of being what he certainly looked like—a vagrant.

Charlie crossed his legs and turned a bland countenance to the girl.

"Square your shoulders," he said, "and throw out your chest."

She obeyed him wonderingly.

"Now take a deep breath," invited Charlie.

She did so.

"Great air, isn't it?" he asked enthusiastically. "Have another?"

"Another what?" she demanded in perplexity.

"Another deep breath," said Charlie. "Go ahead, if you like—when I'm with a girl, I go the limit to show her a good time. That's the way I am."

Her laugh pealed out again.

"I don't think," said she, "he should have gone for a policeman, but for an ambulance, instead. You're not all there, I guess."

Charlie nodded, echoing her laugh.

"Nobody home but the egg, and that's going to beat it," he admitted. "But, seriously," he resumed, throwing his leg chummily over her lap, "don't you like me a little—even if I'm not like the rest of the family?"

She shoved his leg off her knees indignantly.

"How dare you, sir?"

"Now, don't talk as if you were working for me!" Charlie protested, still good-humoredly. "Drop the 'sir,' and call me Charlie. And what do they call *you* at home when they want to let you know dinner's ready?"

"Never mind what my name is," said the girl quickly; "I won't tell you."

"Ah, go on!" urged Charlie, nudging her. "Grace? Emma? Annabelle? Marie? Susanna? Flora? Mildred? Corinne? Katherine? Kerosene——"

She drew away from him stiffly.

"I think you'd better go before he comes back with that policeman," she said unsmilingly.

"The policeman doesn't live," declared Charlie boldly, "who's afraid of me! I mean—but, that is to say, rather than tear myself from your side, little girl, I'd run the risk of facing a thousand policemen!"

Still her stiffness did not relax.

"I won't have you get into trouble on my account," she said grimly, "so you needn't stay."

"You don't like me, then, at all?" asked Charlie anxiously.

"I'm afraid," she nodded coldly, "you have guessed it."

Charlie sighed, and rose. Looking neither to the right nor left, and without a word, he started to walk away from the bench. Carrying his little cane by the end, with its handle hanging down behind him, by accident it hooked around the girl's ankle and he pulled her off the bench to a sitting posture on the walk.

"Help!" she cried out.

Her call was not long unheeded. A man who had been strolling that way along the path broke into a run which quickly brought him to her side. Lifting her to her feet, he glanced from her to Charlie, who was standing near.

"Is he annoying you, madam?" the stranger inquired, with a nod toward Charlie.

"He pulled me off this bench!" the girl indignantly charged.

Charlie opened his lips to explain. Then he shut them again swiftly, and raised his derby to the man, who had reached him in a single stride. The man thrust his face into Charlie's threateningly.

"Well?" he growled.

Charlie coughed behind his hand. He raised his hat again, and turned around to walk off.

The man kicked him in that portion of his baggy trousers which was the fullest.

Without looking around, Charlie retaliated by knocking his hat off with his cane. And then he ambled away from the scene on his heels.

A little farther along the path, he came face to face with the cross-eyed man, who was returning from the unsuccessful search he had made for a policeman.

Charlie knocked his high hat off once more. Then, as the man bent over to pick it up, with the crook of his cane Charlie pulled one of his feet from under him, and left him sprawling there in the middle of the walk, while he waddled on his way.

Five minutes later, the cross-eyed man met the man who had answered the girl's cry for help, and driven Charlie away from the bench, in front of the seat from which the girl had also gone.

The cross-eyed man and the other shook hands, for they were old acquaintances.

"I left a young lady sitting on this bench just a few minutes ago," said the former. "Did you happen to see anything of her?"

"I did," replied his friend. "But it didn't do me any good. She wouldn't let me sit beside her, or talk to her, or anything. She said she was through with men forever. It was all on account of a young fellow who she said had pulled her off this bench by the handle of his cane—he had cured her of the desire for masculine society."

They looked at each other in silence for a moment.

"He tripped me up with his cane!" announced the cross-eyed man darkly.

"He knocked my hat off with it," said his friend.

Then, linking arms, by mutual consent they turned and set off in the direction where Charlie Chaplin had last been seen—to exact the penalty of his many crimes from him.

Charlie, seated alone on another bench where he had dropped down for a few moments' rest, saw them coming. He rose and walked away.

The cross-eyed man and his friend came after him. Aware that flight was hopeless, Charlie stopped and waited for the pair to come up.

He spun round on his heel and launched a blow at the cross-eyed man. It met its mark. He staggered back against his friend, and they both sprawled on the path in a tangle of legs and arms. Charlie, looking down at them as they struggled to free themselves of each other's limbs, tipped his derby to them and strolled away, without a word.

Rounding the bend in the path, Charlie caught sight of two angry women sitting on a bench. They were the wife and daughter of the cross-eyed man. And, having just waked up and found him gone from between them, that accounted for their anger. Charlie stopped in front of the bench on which they sat, and raised his hat, with a smile at the pretty girl.

She smiled back.

"Mother," she said, turning to the older woman beside her, "as long as papa has gone off and left us alone here—probably to follow some girl, too!—suppose we take this young man home with us?"

At her daughter's utterance of the same suspicion that had crossed her own mind as to the reason for her husband's desertion of them on the bench while they had been asleep, the woman's lips tightened.

"That is a good idea," she nodded grimly, "and it's what we'll do."

She smiled cordially at Charlie.

"Won't you come home with us?" she asked him.

Charlie looked at her daughter—she was even prettier than the girl on the other bench had been, he told himself.

"Oh—why, certainly, certainly!" he turned to answer the older woman, with another tip of his hat at her.

The girl rose and took Charlie's arm on one side. Her mother slipped her arm through his on the other. And off they set. Five minutes later, Charlie found himself in a brownstone residence, in a fashionable side street near one of the entrances to the park, and not a little awed by the richness of his surroundings. The cross-eyed man, who had provided this home for his wife and daughter, must have prospered exceedingly in whatever business was his.

"Make yourself right at home!" his wife told Charlie Chaplin, as she and her daughter removed their hats. That reminded Charlie to take off his own, which he had not yet done. He was embarrassed as a boy paying his first visit to a dancing class, in the unexpectedly sumptuous interior of that house. In his confusion, he sat down on top of the girl's hat, which she had dropped in one of the drawing-room chairs.

Charlie got up again—swiftly.

The hat was clinging to the seat of his trousers by the hatpins which he had encountered upon accepting his hostess' invitation to sit down—without looking first to see where he sat.

Charlie reached around behind him, with a martyr's smile at the pretty girl who had remained in the room with him while her mother was occupied in the next—which, from the clink of chinaware and silver that floated from it, appeared to be the dining room—and removed the hat.

"What's the matter?" asked the girl. "Wasn't that chair comfortable? Try this one."

Charlie crossed the room, with a deprecatory smile and a shrug of his shoulders, to the chair she indicated, and seated himself in it. An expression of intense suffering instantly contorted his face. He rose again—having sat down on her mother's hat this time. There were a number of feathers in it, and, with the hat sticking by the hatpins to the seat of his trousers, and the feathers pluming out under his short coat, Charlie looked like a rooster. He tried to pull the hatpins out, and failed.

"Here, let me help you!" offered the girl, aware of his plight.

She took hold of the hat and pulled. Charlie went up on his toes. He pressed his hand to his cheek. Then he inserted the fingers of it in his mouth, and bit on them while the girl continued to pull at the pins that the force with which he had sat down in the chair had driven into him up to the hilt, so to speak. The hat came away, and Charlie sank back on his heels once more. He wiped the cold perspiration from his brow.

"I liked your mother's hat the minute I saw it," he informed the girl, with a wan attempt at a smile; "but I didn't think I'd get so stuck on it that I'd try to take it away with me—like this!"

Her mother appeared at that moment in the doorway of the next room.

"Won't you come and have something to eat?" she invited Charlie.

Charlie's little black mustache took a doleful slant above his mouth, which drooped open. He stood up on his tiptoes, and craned his neck to look by the wife of the cross-eyed man into the dining room behind her. At sight of the table, all set there, and the food upon it, Charlie's woebegone expression deepened.

"Well, I lose!" he said.

Mother and daughter looked blankly at each other and then at him.

"Lose what?" asked the girl.

"The bet that I made with myself that I wouldn't get anything to eat before to-morrow," Charlie answered, with a sorrowful shake of his head. "I hate to lose it, too. For that makes two dollars more I'll have to add to what I already owe myself. I'm afraid to look at myself in the glass when I'm shaving any more, for fear I will threaten to sue me for not paying my debts."

Laughingly the girl and her mother escorted Charlie to the table and seated him there between them. There was a plate of doughnuts before Charlie.

"The ship's going down," said Charlie gayly to the cross-eyed man's wife. "Will you have a life preserver?"

"Please," she assented.

Charlie picked up his fork and thrust it through the hole of one of the doughnuts. Then he brought the fork, empty, around to her plate. He started in surprise, looking from the vacant tines of the fork to the doughnut which should have been there, but wasn't. He tried again to lift one of the doughnuts on the fork by its hole. Then, picking up his knife, he thrust the blade through the hole of a doughnut, twirled it up in the air, and caught it, as it came down, on the knife blade again.

He transferred the doughnut from the knife to the plate of the cross-eyed man's wife, then placed a doughnut on the girl's plate the same way, and served one to himself.

"They're wild things," Charlie remarked, "but they can be trained to come when you call them, by a little patience and skill."

He was just about to take a bite of the doughnut to which he had helped himself, when he put it back on the plate again, untasted, with the doleful expression overspreading his countenance once more.

The front door of the house had closed with a bang.

And, in the next room, a voice which Charlie recognized as that of the cross-eyed man who was the lord and master of the house, rose in tones of angry complaint.

"I leave them on that bench for two minutes," was what Charlie heard him saying, "and when I come back they're gone! That's the way they treat me. I can't turn my back, but they run away!"

Charlie heard the voice of the cross-eyed man's friend, whom he had brought home with him, in the next room.

"Maybe they didn't run away. How do you know they weren't kidnaped?"

The cross-eyed man laughed bitterly.

"I'd like to see the man who would kidnap my wife, with that face of hers!" said he. "I'd like to see him—and shake him by the hand!"

With an apologetic little laugh, Charlie looked around at the cross-eyed man's wife, who sat beside him at the table and could hear every word her husband said as plainly as he could. She rose, with her lips pressed together in a thin line, and marched into the next room.

"You don't think any man would run away with me, do you?" Charlie heard her demand of her husband. "Well, you're wrong. And I can prove it to you."

Charlie looked at the pretty girl beside him. He gave her a weak smile, and then looked anxiously beyond her in the direction of the other door of the dining room, through which he was speculating on his chances of escaping from the house, where he began to feel a conviction stealing over him that he was about to come face to face with Trouble with a capital T, in a very few moments more.

"I'll show you whether I ran away from that bench where you left me, alone or with a man," Charlie heard the cross-eyed man's wife inform him. "Just go into the next room and see who you'll find there."

Charlie rose abruptly from the table.

"Good-by," he whispered to the girl, taking a step on tiptoe toward that other door, "and I'll be sure to write when I get to Texas!"

Then he stopped short, and turned. The cross-eyed man, following his wife's suggestion, had strode into the dining room and discovered Charlie Chaplin there. Instantly he recognized in him the person who had twice knocked his hat off, and tripped him up the same number of times, with his cane in the park. With a mighty roar of wrath, and his arms outspread, he made a dash at Charlie.

Charlie eluded him by running around the table. The cross-eyed man came after him. Charlie dodged back around the table. He was handicapped in the race by his short legs, however; the other almost seized his flying coat tails in one outstretched hand. Charlie attempted to climb over the table. The cross-eyed man grabbed him by one ankle, bringing him down, with a crash, among the china and glassware, and then swept him toward him over the top of the table.

Picking Charlie up in his arms, kicking and squirming, he hurled him through the portières into the next room.

Charlie collided with the cross-eyed man's friend.

Picking himself up, as Charlie, doing likewise, was starting to run away, the other man also recognized him as the author of the attack which had tangled him up with his friend on the park path.

He ran after Charlie, and caught him by the slack of his baggy trousers, thus detaining him in his attempted flight.

Charlie turned around. The other changed his grip to the waistband of his trousers. Charlie, to try to make him let go his hold, whirled round and round the middle of the floor with him in a wild travesty on the maxixe. The cross-eyed man's friend lost his footing—though he kept his grip on the waistband of those trousers. Alas! if they themselves could but have clung as tenaciously to Charlie Chaplin's person. There, was a long-drawn, ripping sound.

And Charlie's trousers came off!

His spindling legs stood revealed in a pair of white cotton tights, which, like the trousers that had hitherto concealed them from view of the world, were several sizes too big for him. A pair of black-and-white striped swimming trunks—that even a gambler would have called loud—encircled his waist. And they, also, were too big for him. Looking something like a ballet dancer and a scarecrow combined, Charlie stood for a moment beside his fallen antagonist, who held his trousers.

And then he turned and ran out of the house.

It was Sunday morning, and the first persons Charlie encountered on his arrival in the street in his pants-less condition were perhaps a hundred or so ladies and gentlemen sedately returning from church.

At sight of Charlie, one or two of the women shrieked, and covered their faces. One or two more fainted quietly against their escorts. Nearly all the rest turned and ran the other way, pulling their husbands, brothers, and sweethearts by the hand with them away from the dangerous proximity of the "lunatic," which was what Charlie appeared to them to be.

But their flight was unnecessary, for Charlie, at sight of them, had likewise turned and run in the opposite direction.

It was the direction of the house out of which he had just dashed. Its door still stood open, with nobody blocking his way upon its threshold. And back into the house, which offered his only avenue of escape, Charlie galloped.

He saw no one in the downstairs hall. But before him he saw something else, and that was the stairway leading up to the second floor of the residence. Two at a time, Charlie mounted those stairs, and burst into a bedroom, where it was his intention to hide until the trouble from which he had escaped—though bereft of his trousers—downstairs should have blown over.

Closing the door of the bedroom softly behind him, Charlie turned—and gasped.

He saw what at first he took to be a young lady in fashionable attire confronting him. A young lady who had neither neck nor face, and whose smart, white toque was thus resting on her shoulders!

Charlie raised his battered derby to her.

"How do you do?" he murmured under his breath. And then he saw, on longer inspection, that it wasn't a young lady at all. It was a dressmaker's form, on which the white toque, white tailor-made suit and white fox fur set, which probably comprised the new costume of the young lady of the house that had just come home, had been hung.

And, with this discovery, another flashed upon Charlie's mind—of the way he might escape from the house, unmolested by its masculine inmates, who thirsted for his blood, and without causing a riot on the street in his present partial costume.

Casting off his derby and his coat, Charlie seized the toque from the form and clapped it on his head. He pulled the dress and fur neck piece and muff from the dummy next, and, five minutes later, clad in the dress and boa, and with his hands thrust into the muff—Charlie Chaplin had become a girl, to all outward appearances!

He strolled, for practice, up and down the room a few times with the proper débutante slouch. And then he opened the door of the bedroom and stepped out into the hall.

He came face to face with the cross-eyed man's pretty daughter, to whom the costume which he had appropriated from the dressmaker's form belonged.

She took one look at Charlie, and burst out laughing. Her mirth increased, as she continued to regard him. She leaned up against the wall, and then weakly slid down along it to a sitting posture on the floor, the tears rolling down her cheeks.

"What's the matter?" Charlie asked her anxiously. "It isn't a good disguise, then—and I thought nobody would recognize me in it!"

"You—you thought," gasped the girl, pointing to his face, "nobody would see your mustache?"

Charlie put up his hand, in surprise, to his upper lip.

"Wait till I get you my father's shaving things," said she, rising from the floor and wiping her eyes. "After you've shaved that off, I think you'll do. Your disguise *is* perfect, all but that. You make a very pretty girl."

With which compliment, she hastened along the hall and entered another room. In a moment or two, she returned with a shaving brush and cup and a razor. Before the mirror of the dressing table in her room, out of which he had come, Charlie removed his mustache, while she looked on. And then, sauntering to and fro for her approval, Charlie went downstairs.

The first person he met there was the cross-eyed man's friend.

And he fell for the charming young lady he took Charlie to be—hard. Charlie, escorted by the infatuated recipient of his shy smiles, eyebrow liftings, and shrugs to a chair in the drawing-room of the house, had hard work to keep his face straight.

"What are you going to be doing to-morrow night?" the cross-eyed man's friend whispered, as he leaned ardently over the back of Charlie's chair.

Charlie choked, and lowered his head.

"Shoeing a horse!" he answered faintly.

But then, realizing that he must get rid of the man in some way so that he could escape from the house, Charlie sank back weakly in the chair.

"Will you get me a glass of water, please?" he requested. "I feel quite woozy in the head!"

With alacrity, the cross-eyed man's friend left the room upon the errand. Charlie rose from the chair. And then he sat down in it again. The cross-eyed man himself entered.

At sight of Charlie—whom he was also fooled into taking for a pretty girl—he looked back cautiously through the portières that separated the drawing-room from the one in which he had just left his wife, and then he hastened to Charlie's side.

Dropping on his knees at his side, he breathed fervently:

"Tell me where you came from, you beautiful angel!"

His friend, returning at that moment to find the master of the house paying court to the supposed girl he had just left, tiptoed forward and poured the glass of water, which Charlie had asked him to bring, over the other's head, as he knelt there on the floor.

The cross-eyed man rose, spluttering.

"You keep away from my girl!" his friend warned him angrily.

"She's not yours!" the other retorted, with as much heat. "She's mine!"

Charlie, in the rôle of peacemaker, intervened.

"Now, wait!" said he coyly. "I'll be fair to both of you. You can each have a kiss—on my cheek, mind! Now, one of you stand on one side of me. And one on the other. When I say 'three,' you can both kiss me at the same time. Are you ready? All right, then—one, two, *three!*"

Charlie ducked and stepped back. And the two men, eagerly bringing their heads forward to imprint the promised kiss upon Charlie's cheek, kissed each other, instead.

The cross-eyed man, angrily seizing his equally infuriated friend, picked him up bodily by the back of his coat collar and the slack of his trousers, and ran him out of the house.

Then he returned to Charlie.

Dropping down on his knees beside him once more, he grasped the hem of his skirt and pressed it to his lips. And at that moment his wife and daughter entered the room behind him. His wife, not being in on the joke, was likewise fooled into thinking that it was a young and beautiful girl at whose feet she saw her husband kneeling. With lowering brows, she was on the point of interrupting the ardent love scene by striding forward to seize her spouse by the hair and pull him back from the "charmer." Her daughter, silently convulsed at the spectacle her father presented on his knees beside Charlie, checked her.

"Wait, mother," she whispered. "It's all a mistake—as you'll understand in a minute, I guess."

It was less than that brief space of time, when the revelation of Charlie's masquerade came, not only to the cross-eyed man's wife, but to the latter as well.

Charlie, discovering that the man was kissing the hem of his skirt, had started to walk simperingly away. The man held on to his skirt. And it came off in his hands, leaving him staring in wide-eyed amazement at a pair of white cotton tights that were too big for the legs they clothed. In an instant he sprang up with rage smoldering in his eyes. He had recognized Charlie; and, closing his fist, he began to roll up his sleeve above it.

Charlie, who was the only one in the room that did not know his skirt had come off, was strolling up and down the floor, with his eyebrows coyly lifting and his shoulders shrugging overtime.

The cross-eyed man drew back his arm and was just about to launch a blow at his unsuspecting head.

His daughter, running forward, caught his arm.

"Ah, spare him, father!" she declaimed melodramatically. "I love him!"

Her father turned hesitatingly and looked at Charlie. That young man, with dawning terror in his countenance, was looking down at his undraped legs. He straightened, and met the cross-eyed man's gaze fixed upon him. With a weak smile, Charlie raised the toque on his head at him. The girl squeezed her father's arm, to which she still held on appealingly.

"Please, daddy!" she urged.

With a shrug of resignation, the man took his daughter's hand in one of his. He held out the other to Charlie, and Charlie placed his hand in it. Then her father was about to bring their hands together, à la the final moving-picture scene in which the hero gets the heroine, but abruptly the thought of all that Charlie had done to him surging across his memory, he changed his mind.

He hauled off and knocked Charlie sprawling across the room.

"Get out of here!" the cross-eyed man roared after him, as Charlie, picking himself up, was dashing for the door. "Get out of the city! Get out of this country—or I won't be responsible for the consequences!"

And Charlie, running up the street with a girl's hat on his head, a girl's waist and jacket on the upper part of his body, and nothing but a pair of white cotton tights on the lower part, mused to himself:

"I'll get *into* the observation ward of some hospital, if I'm seen in this rig, that's what I'll do! And there's no hope of my not being seen, either. There's only one thing for me to do."

And Charlie, at the same dead run, turned the next corner in the direction of the river—as the one place left for him to hide his untrousered legs.

Work

THE house looked as though an earthquake had struck it—and an earthquake with a bent for playing practical jokes, at that. The dining-room table stood in the hall; the chairs stood on top of the table; pictures, instead of hanging on the walls, were stacked on the floor; rugs, instead of lying on the floor, were rolled up and leaning against the walls; curtains and portières were folded and lying on top of the pictures. Everything was topsy-turvy.

Yet it was no earthquake that had wrought this nightmarish upheaval. It was the work of human hands—planned and executed by the lady of the house, with the assistance of the maid, an hour before the master of the household rose.

The paper hangers were coming. So the lord and master of the dwelling was informed when he gazed, in round-eyed bewilderment, upon the dismantled dining room and the confusion in which his household goods were piled up in the hall without.

"You'll have to eat your breakfast in the kitchen," his wife informed him preoccupiedly. "And you can get it yourself. You'll find the coffeepot on the shelf, eggs in the refrigerator, and bread in the box. Gladys and I haven't any more than time to get the things out of the parlor before the men come."

Her husband roared—as husbands, under the circumstances, are wont to do.

"I don't want my breakfast in the kitchen!" he emphatically declared. "I don't want to get it myself—for one thing, I've got an important engagement at the office this morning, and I can't spare the time. Have Gladys get my——"

His wife waved him imperiously toward the kitchen.

"Gladys is going to help me clear out the parlor," she announced in a tone which implied that the matter was settled; "and we've got to hurry. It's after eight o'clock, and the men should have been here three-quarters of an hour ago."

Up the principal business thoroughfare of the city, toward that house, Izzy A. Wake, painter and paper hanger, was hastening even then, with his assistant.

Rather, it was the assistant who was hastening. In a pushcart that was additionally loaded with one step-ladder, one two-by-four plank, one gallon bucket of paste, with brush, six rolls of wall paper, and other paraphernalia of the painting and paper-hanging trade too numerous for detailed enumeration, sat Izzy A. Wake, the owner of the outfit, in person—two hundred odd pounds of it. With the handle of the cart gripped in both hands and straining against his puny chest, his assistant puffed and struggled to draw the load along.

On the assistant's bushy hair was a derby of antiquated design, and dented, weather-beaten aspect. Buttoned tight about his unheroic chest and narrow shoulders was a coat that must have been cut originally by a tailor who feared a shortage in the woolen-goods market. What the coat lacked in material, however, was more than made up for by the trousers below it. They hung upon their wearer in folds, wrinkles, pleats, billows, and festoons. They were not alone too big for him—they would have lapped over if three other persons besides himself had stood in them.

On his feet were a pair of shoes, either of which could have been hung up as a sign outside a shoe dealer's store, and with the perfect assurance that it would be seen twenty blocks away.

The shoes needed a shine—had needed it, and gone without that need being filled, for years, it seemed—and as their wearer ran in them, pulling the pushcart with its load of painters' supplies and his employer along the busy street, the turned-up toes of those shoes were pointed almost at exact right angles to each other.

Charlie Chaplin paused to recover his breath; but at once his little bamboo cane, in the hand of his employer who rode behind him, descended on his back.

"Git ap!" ordered the boss paper hanger. "Don't you know we're late, as it is? Move along—as fast as you can travel!"

Charlie Chaplin's little black mustache took a woebegone slant on his upper lip, and he lifted his eyes hopelessly to heaven. Seizing the handle of the pushcart once more, he obeyed his employer's command. But as fast as Charlie could travel was not a very high rate of speed—due to the fact that he relied solely upon his heels as a means of locomotion.

Motormen clanged their bells at him. Chauffeurs honked their auto horns in his ears. Drivers of trucks and delivery wagons shouted anathema upon his head. He was blocking the traffic.

His employer, spying from the pushcart the approach of a brass-buttoned and blue-uniformed custodian of the law, hooked Charlie by the back of the coat collar with the handle of his little cane, bringing him to a halt.

"Turn into this street," he ordered Charlie. "We'll take the short cut."

Obediently Charlie swung the cart around, and drew it across the car tracks of the main thoroughfare into the mouth of the side street his employer had indicated. Looking up the street before him, Charlie groaned. It was a hill—steep, almost, as the side of a house. And this was what his boss had called a short cut!

"Git ap!" ordered the paper hanger, slapping him across the shoulder once more with the cane.

Charlie began the toilsome ascent of the hill. The steep incline added to the weight of the cart behind him. A third of the way up he came to a pause. But only for an instant. In vain he tried to keep his feet. The cart began to pull him back faster than he could pull the cart forward. In vain his employer beat him with the cane, urging him on. The cart, the paper hanger, and Charlie Chaplin slid down the hill.

The cart rolled across the car tracks of the main thoroughfare. Unconscious of his danger, Charlie started to draw it back across them just as a trolley came whizzing along.

The motorman shouted, and jumped up and down on the gong, waving his arms. Charlie paid no heed to him. And on the car came—bent, it seemed, on smashing the pushcart, with its load, into kindling wood, in another moment. The rear of the cart cleared the car tracks just as the fender of the trolley went swishing by.

The outfit had missed destruction by the margin of a hair.

Up the hill once more Charlie tugged and pushed the cart. He got two-thirds of the way up the ascent this time before the law of gravity began to exert itself again. Frantically Charlie's feet pawed the ground. He struggled gamely to secure a foothold—gamely, but to no avail. Back the cart pulled him, gripping the bar between its two handles, to the thoroughfare at the bottom of that steep side street once more, and onto its car tracks.

A second trolley was approaching, nearer than the first had been; but again Charlie paid no heed to it, dragging the cart back onto the tracks again, and squarely into the path of the onrushing car.

The second motorman clanged the bell, shouting. With his eyes fixed straight before him, his whole weight thrown forward, Charlie was serenely bent on tackling the hill in front of him a third time. The trolley was now only ten feet away, and coming at a twenty-mile-an-hour clip. But for all the attention he paid to its clanging bell and shouting motorman, Charlie might have been alone in the middle of the Sahara Desert, instead of standing five feet—now it was only three—away from sudden death under the wheels of the car.

This time, Charlie assaulted the hill on "the high," as it were. Running on his heels, he hauled the cart up the incline at a brisk pace. And this time, encouraged by the shouts of his employer, he succeeded in reaching the summit.

He had not dragged the cart forward another block, however, before the paper hanger again pulled him to a halt by inserting the crook of the bamboo cane down the back of his coat collar and giving it a yank.

"Good morning, Mr. Hemingway!" the painter greeted a man with mortar on his shoes and a hod over his shoulder, the sight of whom had caused him to bring Charlie Chaplin to a halt. "On your way to work?"

"Right!" assented the hodcarrier, with a lugubrious shake of his head. "Bad 'cess, and double bad, to the man that invented it, too!"

"Hand me your hod," said Charlie's employer heartily. "I'll put it in the cart with my things, and you get up here on the seat beside me. If you're going my way, you might as well ride along with me. It'll rest you—go ahead, there, Sylvester!" this to Charlie, as the paper hanger's friend, the hodcarrier, accepting the invitation with alacrity, added the burden of his not-inconsiderable weight to the load poor Charlie was hauling.

Charlie, sighing, plodded onward. Again his eyes were fixed straight ahead, as he threw his weight against the handle of the cart. Thus it was that he did not see the pitfall that yawned literally for his feet. He was approaching an open manhole in the street. He raised one foot; it hovered for an instant above that round, black opening——

The paper hanger and his friend the hodcarrier were deep in an animated discussion of ways and means whereby the semblance of having put in an eight-hour day of hard work could be given by the expenditure of but one hour or less. From this improving conversation they were roused abruptly by the fact that the cart had stopped with the same suddenness.

They turned simultaneously to look for Charlie Chaplin—and saw him not.

He was gone. He had vanished, disappeared, as utterly as though—what indeed was the case—the ground had opened to swallow him.

The hodcarrier climbed quickly down on one side of the cart. The paper hanger followed his example on the other.

"That's odd!" said the painter, staring blankly at the vacant space between the handles of the cart where Charlie should have been. "He—he isn't there!"

"It's a fact," agreed the hodcarrier, scratching his ear in perplexity, "he ain't. Now, where can he have gone to?"

In an endeavor to find the answer to that question, the hodcarrier went to the rear of the cart, bent down with his hands on his knees, and looked under it. Charlie's boss joined him in the attitude and occupation.

"Maybe," the hodcarrier suggested, straightening and laying hold of the back of the cart, which was tilted above his head, "he's in here among the ladder and the buckets and the paper and things. Let's take a look."

As both seized the rear of the cart, and pulled it down, Charlie Chaplin, still clinging to the bar between the handles, was lifted out of the manhole. He stepped across it and dragged the cart forward.

And that was how the hodcarrier, loosing his hold on the back of the cart as he felt it start ahead, and just as he was borne over the manhole down which Charlie had temporarily dropped from view, came to leave the paper hanger and his outfit at that point in the journey.

"We've done him a favor," Charlie's employer remarked, gazing down into the hole through which his friend had gone. "He can bring a suit against the city, for leaving this manhole open. And, if I know Percy Hemingway, that's what he'll *do*. No more work for him for the next three years! He'll be too busy pushing his lawsuit for damages suffered in body and feelings, by shooting eight feet down into this hole and landing on both feet at the bottom. We don't need to worry about him. Come on—let's get to that house, before we're any later!"

They were only an hour and a half behind time, when Charlie brought the paper hanger's outfit and its owner to a halt in the yard of the house whose redecorating the painter had contracted to do at union rates, plus all the speed of which he was capable.

The ride there, it seemed, had fatigued Charlie's employer. He descended, with frequent groans, from the cart, and drew two black leather articles from his pockets. They were wrist straps. He handed them to Charlie, who adjusted them on the boss paper hanger's wrists, while the latter stood listlessly waiting. Then Charlie's employer lifted his arms above his head and yawned. After which Charlie removed the black leather straps from his wrists, and the paper hanger went into the house to arrange for the starting of the day's work.

Charlie Chaplin, left alone in the yard, leaned up against the side of the cart and groped in the pockets of his short coat.

"I've been working like a horse," he commented to himself, "and I guess I'm entitled to smoke a cigarette."

Charlie put the cigarette, which he had found in one pocket, between his lips. He struck a match along a fold of his loose-fitting trousers, and had just lifted the flame—when he dropped match and cigarette both, with a disconsolate sigh.

"Chauncey!" his boss called to him from the house.

From the cart Charlie took the stepladder and succeeded at last in getting it tucked under one arm. He gathered up the plank under the other. Then, with the paste bucket and brush in one hand, and the rolls of wall paper gripped by the cord that bound them together in the other, he waddled obediently into the house, with his battered derby perched on top of his bushy hair.

Mr. Izzy A. Wake sat in the parlor, where Charlie found him with the mistress of the house and her maid, far down on his spine in one upholstered chair, with his feet in the seat of another. He was smoking a cigarette, of the "roll-your-own" kind that is favored by men who own their own yachts, embassy attachés with red silk bands across the front of their evening-dress shirts—and paper hangers.

"Ethelbert," he addressed Charlie, with a languid wave of the hand that held the cigarette—"help the dames clear out this room. I think I'll take a little snooze while you're doin' it. I was worryin' about my Wall Street stocks last night, and I don't believe I slept more'n forty winks the livelong night through!"

Charlie Chaplin, while he listened to his employer, was not looking at him.

He was looking at the maid.

Gladys was worth looking at. Charlie, flashing her one of his irresistible smiles—as friendship-compelling as the wagging of a puppy's tail—tipped his hat to her by the back of the brim. And the maid, behind her mistress' back, returned the smile.

In a laudable, if unthinking, desire to appear well in her eyes, Charlie turned and seized the piano as the first article to remove from the parlor in obedience to his employer's orders.

"Filbert!"

The boss paper hanger addressed him reprovingly. He pointed to a vase, about three inches high, that stood on the mantelpiece.

"Let go o' that piano! Do you want to lay yourself up? I've spoken to you about overworkin' before, I guess! Take out that vause. And, after you've come back and rested, you can take out the mate to it, there on the other end of the mantelpiece."

Charlie—the "vause," as his boss called it, in his hand—turned to leave the room with it. And then he stopped. Stopped and wriggled his shoulders embarrassedly. His eye had just caught sight of something else. It was a statuette—Venus rising on a point of order, or something—and, as he looked at the statuette, which stood on a table beside him, Charlie's face turned red as a beet.

He turned around and faced the door. Then he looked back over his shoulder again at the statuette. He lifted his hand an inch to touch it; and then, pulling his hand back by the handle of his little bamboo cane, he shrugged and walked out of the room.

He was greeted by an explosion that shook the house from cellar to garret.

"It's my husband!" gasped the lady of the house, rushing by him. "He's trying to get his own breakfast, and that's the third time in the last hour that that stove has exploded!"

Charlie Chaplin, guided by curiosity, followed her to the kitchen.

There he found the master of the dwelling ruefully looking up at the ceiling, where were stuck the remains of two fried eggs, surrounded by a brown stippling of coffee grounds—the spot to which his breakfast had flown from the top of the stove, beyond recovery.

The head of the household bore a smudge of stove polish on one cheek, while his eye on the other side was completely surrounded by a circle of the same sable substance.

"Will you have Gladys——" he began, in a tone of exasperation held in restraint.

"Wait, John!" hastily put in his wife. "Perhaps this man can fix the stove. Do you think you can?"

She addressed Charlie Chaplin. Thus appealed to, Charlie lifted his arms and let them fall again to his sides, in a gesture significant of the fact that he felt what was asked of him to be a thing childishly simple of accomplishment.

Charlie approached the stove, drawing out a match. He struck the match and applied the flame to one of the stove's burners. Then gingerly he turned on the gas. It lit, without a single splutter, and burned steadily.

Charlie turned away, repeating his indifferent gesture.

"There you are!" said he.

The next second there was another booming explosion. And Charlie, who had been facing the open door of the kitchen, was wafted through it and back into the parlor. Picking himself up, he found that the maid and his employer between them had emptied the room of all its movable furnishings during his absence. The boss paper hanger was ready to begin the task of papering the walls.

He had opened the stepladder and placed it beside one of the room's four walls; and now he rested one end of the plank on one of the ladder's upper steps, and gave the other end of it to Charlie to hold on his shoulder.

Then, the bucket of paste in his hand, with another yawn, Charlie's employer mounted the ladder and seated himself on the board, with the pail of paste beside him.

The maid smiled at Charlie.

"Lovely weather we're having, isn't it?" he addressed her conversationally, with one end of the plank on which sat his employer resting on his shoulder.

"Yes," giggled Gladys; and came to his side.

"What are you going to be doing a year from next Fourth of July?"

"A year from——" she began, puzzled.

"Yes; I expect to have two dollars laid by out of the wages I'm getting in this job by that time," explained Charlie, "and I thought I'd like to take you out for a good time then."

The maid laughed.

"Why do you want to take me out?" she inquired archly. "I'll bet you know lots of girls."

"But none as pretty as you!" protested Charlie; and in the fervor of his declaration he forgot himself, and took a step nearer to her side, moving out from under the end of the plank.

The plank fell with a crash, sending the paper hanger to the floor. The bucket of paste landed with him—literally so; for it had dropped upside down on his head.

Charlie essayed to go to his employer's assistance. He stepped in a slippery mass of the paste that had splattered on the floor, and measured his length at the paper hanger's side. Getting to his feet with difficulty, Charlie tried to stay on them. The area surrounding the boss painter—

who sat bolt upright and speechless, with that overturned pail of paste on his head—was like a sliding pond. Charlie fell down twice more before he succeeded in getting the other by the hand and pulling him up.

Then they both fell down again. Charlie rose, and his feet flew back and forth on the slippery floor under him as a skater's—without moving him off that one spot. At last, regaining his balance, he left his employer sitting there, and removed the bucket from his head.

The paper hanger looked like a man who had run head first into an open can of ice cream. Paste filled his eyes, his ears, and his nostrils. His hair was full of it. Charlie, picking up the brush and placing the bucket before him, removed about two pounds and a half of the sticky stuff from the other's countenance with a sweep of the brush, and deposited it in the waiting pail.

He had succeeded in removing, in this way, about half of the paste from his employer's head and face, which his own carelessness had placed there, when the maid reëntered the parlor.

"The room upstairs is ready now," she informed Charlie, "if you want to go up and start papering it."

Turning from his boss, Charlie dropped the brush into the bucket of paste and lifted it in one hand, picking up a roll of wall paper in the other, and obediently followed the maid from that room to the one she pointed out to him on the second floor of the house.

Whistling a tune, off key, while he worked, Charlie tore off a long, ragged strip from the roll of wall paper he had brought with him, and lathered it on one side with paste. Then, forgetting that he had done so, he smeared it with paste on the other.

The paper curled up in his hands. It seemed possessed. The harder he struggled to get rid of it, the more it tangled and twisted and writhed—like a thing alive, and full of mocking perversity—around him. He managed to get it off one hand, only to find that it was then stuck fast to the other. At length, perspiring and wild-eyed, he managed to tear the last of the paper from him, and added it to the scraps that littered the floor at his feet.

Then, breathlessly, he sat down on the side of the bed to rest.

"How did you come to be a paper hanger?" asked Gladys, who had been watching him.

"It's a sad story," said Charlie in a tone in keeping with that introduction. "Sit down here beside me, and I'll tell you all about it. Years and years ago—I think it must have been at least two weeks from last Wednesday—I happened to see an advertisement in the paper."

At that moment there had come into the house downstairs, without the formality of ringing the front-door bell, the foreign musician who lived alone in the house next door.

His card, which he handed to prospective piano pupils, bore the information that he was M. Edouard Chateaubriac, late of the Conservatoire of Marseilles; and he was more kinds of a nut than you will find at the grocery in a pound marked "mixed."

As evidence of it, he had fallen head over heels in love with the lady of that house; and, moreover, he imagined that she was in love with him.

It was a combination of the artistic temperament and the French nature—a "mixed" nut, that's right.

Stealing on tiptoe down the hall to the door of the kitchen, M. Chateaubriac saw the object of his adoration standing there—alone, as he thought. He did not know—how could he, for he could not see him?—that her husband was underneath the stove, where he had crawled to see what was the matter with the "double-dot, dashed thing," as he called it.

"Ah-h, *ma cherie!*" gurgled the Frenchman in tones of rapture; and he rushed forward and clasped the good lady in his arms.

At that moment, the husband crawled out from under the stove. He took one look at his wife in another man's embrace, and ran to get his gun.

"I saw an advertisement in the paper," Charlie Chaplin was continuing his "sad story" to the maid in the room upstairs. "It offered a good, steady job to a young man who was not afraid to work. That is one thing I have never been afraid to do. Stealing—for fear of getting caught and going to jail, yes. Or fighting, and rough things like that, for fear of getting hurt, I've been afraid to do. But not to work. There have been too many poems written and songs sung about the virtue of honest toil. Nobody would deride me for going to work. It would be a shock to the family, who would feel that I had disgraced them—but, there; we won't go into that. The story is sad enough as it is, without making it any sadder by telling you about my family. Where was I?"

"You weren't anywhere," said the maid, somewhat sharply. "You hadn't got any place yet."

"I'm not boring you, am I?" asked Charlie Chaplin anxiously. "Well, I answered the advertisement. And you see me now. Didn't I tell you that it was a sad story?"

"But what's sad about it?" demanded the maid.

"Why, the advertisement was for this job. And I got it. You don't want anything sadder than that, do you? At least, *I* don't, knowing what I have to put up with."

Three shots rang out on the stillness of the house at that moment.

The master of the dwelling had returned to the kitchen with his gun to open fire upon the foreign musician in whose arms he had seen his wife. Where two of those shots landed, Charlie Chaplin did not know. But he was personally able to account for one. He bounded up from the side of the bed, clutching at his coat tails.

In a single leap, he had crossed the room and was frantically lathering the wall with the paste brush.

The door beside him flew open, and in stalked his employer. The boss paper hanger's eyes, inflamed from the paste, of which he had but just now succeeded in freeing them, turned a deeper red with wrath as they rested on Charlie Chaplin.

"So here you are!" roared Charlie's boss, above the rattle of pistol shots that rang through the house, as its infuriated owner pursued the foreign piano teacher, whom he mistook for a home wrecker. "You dropped that plank on purpose, and let that paste bucket come down on my head! I'm going to teach you a lesson you won't for— *Glup!*"

He ended thus abruptly. Charlie had dipped the brush in the pail of paste at his side, and let him have it full in the face.

As the paper hanger fell back through the door, the fleeing Frenchman burst into the room. Charlie sent him back with a blow of the full paste brush between the eyes, too.

The owner of the house ran in, firing the revolver in his hand into the air as he did so. Charlie presented him with a faceful of paste, also, and then ducked to avoid a bullet from the gun, and ran out of the room.

Downstairs he raced, two at a time, with the paper hanger in pursuit.

The Frenchman ran after him.

And the husband pursued the wild-haired musician.

As the trio ran into the kitchen, there was an explosion that was worse than any of the others that had gone before it.

The paper hanger went flying out of one window.

The Frenchman followed suit through another.

And the owner of the residence shot through a third.

The lady of the house and the maid, covering their ears, ran out of the front door.

There was only one left inside the house—and what of him?

One minute passed. Then two. And then, slowly, the oven door opened, and out of the stove looked Charlie Chaplin—where he had hidden to escape from his pursuers.

"Well," said Charlie Chaplin, with an emphatic nod of his head, "I agree with the hodcarrier: Bad 'cess, and double bad, to the man who invented—work!"

The Champion

CHARLIE CHAPLIN looked down at his faithful bulldog. Charlie had found something to eat, and he wanted to see if the dog was as glad as he was. The something was a frankfurter and a roll; and, as Charlie Chaplin lifted it to his lips, he was about to take the first mouthful he had had in two days. Then he lowered the sandwich, while a woebegone look settled on his face. He glanced down at the dog, then to right and left, and then down at the dog again. Removing the frankfurter from the roll, he held it down for the dog to take the first bite.

They were pals, Charlie Chaplin and his bulldog. For that reason, he offered him the frankfurter before he ate any of it. But the dog refused to touch it.

"What's the matter?" asked Charlie. "You don't recognize a departed relative in it, do you? Take a bite!"

Still the dog refused to do so. With a nod of sudden understanding, Charlie reached into his vest pocket and produced a pinch of salt, which he sprinkled on the end of the frankfurter. Then the dog accepted it. While he held the frankfurter down for the dog to chew, Charlie shook the beer keg that stood beside him, to see if there was anything in it. Unable to judge from that test, he made another. Lowering his little bamboo cane into the bunghole, he drew it out, to discover that it was as dry as he was himself. The barrel was empty.

Charlie swung the cane rapidly around by its handle, the woebegone look returned to his face. He tipped his hat to the keg, and sniffed forlornly. Looking down at the dog, he found him in the act of eating up the last morsel of the frankfurter that remained between his fingers.

Charlie let him have it all, and turned his own attention to the empty roll. He took one bite of it slowly. And then a second, slower still. Then, placing the rest of the roll in the inside pocket of his coat for future reference, he picked up the yard or so of clothesline that formed the dog's leash, and rose.

"Here," said Charlie Chaplin to himself, "I'm a bright young man, who ought to be able to go out and find a square meal somewhere. I'm not going to take the edge off my appetite with any more plain bread. The world owes me one-third of a day's living, anyway—one meal, and I'm going to start out and collect it. Come, Theophilus."

Off up the street, Charlie Chaplin waddled on his heels. And, as he went, he tapped the dog beside him frequently with his little cane, swinging it around behind him for the purpose, so that the bow-legged, heavy-jawed, and fierce-eyed "bull" might not feel that he was being neglected.

Before a high board fence, Charlie stopped. There were two signs displayed on it. One of these read:

"Training quarters of Spike Dugan, world's welterweight champion."

And the other, on the door which was set into the fence, bore the information:

"Sparring partners who can take a punch wanted."

Charlie read both signs. Then he read the second one again. He aimed a blow at his chest—and missed. On the second attempt, he succeeded in striking himself a blow which gave forth a hollow sound, as of a button dropping on a drum, due to his extreme emptiness.

"I took it," he mused. "That proves I can qualify for the job. This is as good a place as any to earn the price of a meal. I guess I'll go in and take a few more punches—as well as anything else I can find that isn't nailed down."

As he started toward the door, Charlie tripped on something. It was a horseshoe. He stooped and picked it up. Then, putting the horseshoe in his pocket, he opened the door in the fence and stepped into the yard beyond it.

He found three applicants for the job of sparring partner already waiting on a bench before him. As he walked over to join them, leading his bulldog by the clothesline, Charlie flashed them his smile of ready good-fellowship, and tipped his battered derby to them. But they were all too deeply engrossed in what they were doing to pay any attention to him.

One was a young man who would have had one of the finest chest developments in the world if his stomach had been shoved up a foot or so. He was looking at a photograph of his mother, while the tears rolled down his cheeks, as he listened to the sounds which floated out into the yard from the adjoining gymnasium.

The sounds would have led one to believe that somebody was building a packing case, inside. The resounding *thwacks* which shattered the air were not hammer blows, however, but the impact of the gloved fists of Spike Dugan, the welterweight champion of the world, on the bag he was punching within the gym.

The second young man, who was six feet tall and weighed perhaps one hundred and ten pounds, as he listened to those mighty thuds of leather against leather, played a castanet accompaniment to them with his knees. He was looking straight before him into space, with an expectant expression on his face—but he did not appear especially pleased over what he expected to receive.

The third young man who sat waiting on the bench was seemingly undisturbed by the ominous sounds from the gym. He was a bullet-headed youth with an undershot jaw, and in a sweater and cap, and his jaw was set while he aimed a succession of jabs, upper-cuts, and right and left hooks at an imaginary spot in the air on which his eyes were fixed.

Charlie sat down beside him, and glanced deprecatingly at him out of the corner of his eye. The bullet-headed youth struck him on the ear. Charlie's hat slipped forward over his eyes, and he righted it again. Another of the blows the sweatered one was aiming at the spot in the air at which he glowered from under beetling brows knocked Charlie's hat askew again—either intentionally or by accident.

"Aim at me," Charlie suggested, while he straightened his hat once more, "and you may hit that spot out there in the air that you're looking at. You seem to be wild to-day, Marquard."

Not looking around at him, the tough-looking young man delivered this strange rejoinder out of the corner of his mouth, punctuated with vicious hooks and uppercuts at the imaginary opponent before him.

"Kid Brophy, t'ree roun's, Boston, K. O. Jumbo Miller, Milwaukee, ten roun's, no decision, but I had it on 'im all de way. C. O. D. Hershfield, Palace A. C, N' York, K. O. Dan de Dago, Black's Gymnasium, same place, K. O. Dat's me record, kid—me record. I'm one tough guy. Wanna start anyt'ing wid me?"

Charlie wriggled his shoulders, laughed, and moved along the bench out of reach of the other's gloved fists. The three aspirants for the position of human punching bag to the champion prize fighter had all been given boxing gloves; but these had not yet been brought out to Charlie. Nobody from within the gym had so far discovered that he was there.

"The only thing I could start with you," Charlie told the tough young man flatteringly, "would be a foot race. A fellow with your record as a scrapper—I'd run if you put up your dukes at me."

The sweatered youth nodded grimly.

"Dat's what yuh'd wanna do," he stated. " 'Cause if I ever hit yuh, dere'd be not'in' left uh yuh t' scrape up fer a fun'ral. I'm a hard guy—hard as nails; get me?"

Before Charlie could reply, there was an interruption. It came in the person of Spike Dugan's handler in chief, who entered the yard from the gymnasium. He stopped in front of Charlie.

"Lookin' fer a job as sparrin' partner?" he asked.

"Yes," said Charlie. "What does it pay?"

"Yuh'll git a dime fer every time Spike Dugan hits yuh. Dat's so yuh'll try to last long enough to give him a good work-out. De more punishment yuh c'n stand before he knocks yuh out, de more money yuh'll make—see?"

"And what do I get for hitting him?" asked Charlie. "A good cigar, or something?"

"Say," said the champion's handler scornfully, "if yuh c'n lay yer gloves onto Spike, when he starts after yuh, yuh'll do better'n I think yuh can from yer looks. What d'ye do fer a livin' when yuh're workin'? Tend bar?"

"No," answered Charlie, "you see, it's this way: A beautiful young lady married an old millionaire for his money. She did it for my sake. When he dies, she'll get all his money. Then she's going to marry me, and I'll be fixed for life. I'm waiting for him to die. But in the meantime I'm looking for a chance to earn the price of a meal."

"Put on dese gloves," said the trainer shortly, handing Charlie a pair that were sadly the worse for wear, "an' come on inside an' let Spike look yuh over. We'll see whether yer jaw'll stand a wallop as well as it does de strain uh lyin'."

Charlie Chaplin put on the gloves and followed the fighter's handler into the gymnasium. Spike Dugan, having finished with the punching bag—literally, for it hung like a squeezed-dry orange in its frame where the pugilist's mighty blows had dented and finally burst it—was pacing the floor, with his chest expanded under a faded blue jersey, impatient, it seemed, to make a fresh conquest with his fists.

"Who's de tramp?" he inquired, looking Charlie over.

"Dis guy," explained the champion's trainer, "ain't no tramp. He's a guy dat's got a swell queen stuck on him. She's married to a millionaire, an' when he dies de gal collects his cush an' toins it over to him. Dat's who *he* is."

Spike Dugan nodded soberly.

"De king uh de kidders," he commented. "I getcha. Well, young fella"—this to Charlie—"let's see what kind of a jaw yuh got."

He tilted Charlie Chaplin's head to an angle that suited him, and then tapped him on the chin. Charlie winced. The champion hit him again. Charlie turned his head around to another angle, of his own accord.

"They're all loose on that side," said he. "Now take a whack at the other, and see if you can make the rest of my teeth leave their happy home among the gums."

Spike Dugan obligingly tapped Charlie a couple of times on that side of the jaw. Then he turned to his handler.

"He'll do, I guess," he remarked. "Lead 'im back to de slaughter pen, and send in de others, one at a time."

Charlie, back on the bench in the yard, watched the fat young man go into the gymnasium. Then he saw him come back again. He was brought out into the yard by Spike Dugan's trainer, who dumped him down on the bench like a sack of meal. It was the skinny youth's turn next. He returned in the arms of the trainer even sooner than the other. He, too, had been knocked out. Spike Dugan's handler dumped him unceremoniously down on top of the fat young man, who lay, still unconscious, beside Charlie on the bench.

Hooking the handle of his little bamboo cane through the arm of the first senseless aspirant for the job of sparring partner to the great Spike Dugan, Charlie Chaplin pulled him over to make room for the other on the bench.

Then it was the tough-looking young man's turn. When he came out, it was on a stretcher carried by two handlers of the welterweight prize fighter. Charlie looked from him to the fat youth and then at the skinny young man beside him. He coughed apologetically. Reaching into his pocket, he brought forth the horseshoe. There was a hole in one of the battered pair of boxing gloves that had been given him, and into it Charlie Chaplin thrust the horseshoe. Then Spike Dugan's handler in chief beckoned to him to come into the gymnasium and get his.

"This way for trouble," said Charlie to the two handlers with the stretcher.

And, rising, he marched at their head into the gymnasium. Spike Dugan was standing in a careless attitude in the center of the floor.

Charlie Chaplin, walking to his side, struck an attitude of equal carelessness, with his ridiculous feet crossed. How it happened was all but too quick for the eye to follow. Suddenly Charlie uncrossed his feet, his right hand shot out, and there was Spike Dugan sprawling on the floor.

The horseshoe under the glove had caught the champion welterweight of the world on the point of the jaw, and knocked him out as neatly as he had done the trick to the others.

"Holy mackerel!" gasped the champion's trainer, staring down at his fallen employer in awe. "He's—he's knocked him kickin'! An' wid one punch! De little shrimp!"

Charlie beckoned. with a lordly gesture, to the stretcher carriers who had accompanied him into the gymnasium.

"Take him away," he ordered, nodding toward the vanquished prize fighter on the floor, "and put him out in the yard with the rest of the victims."

But at that moment Spike sat up. He laid his glove gingerly on the lump the size of a duck egg, which the horseshoe had raised on his jaw. And then, looking up at Charlie, his thick brows drew together in a ferocious scowl.

"Dat was a lucky punch yuh slipped over on me, kid," he announced, scrambling to his feet. "But mebbe yuh won't t'ink it was so lucky in about a minnit from now. I'll knock yer block off yuh fer dat!"

As he spoke, he swung for Charlie Chaplin's head. Charlie ducked. And the next moment he had knocked Spike Dugan down again with a blow of the horseshoe-weighted glove. The prize fighter leaped to his feet and ran out of the gym, bellowing for mercy, and Charlie ran after him.

He chased the thoroughly cowed "pug" clear out of the gymnasium yard, and then he returned to it to be lifted up on the shoulders of Spike Dugan's trainer and handlers.

"Yuh're de champeen now!" the handler in chief enthusiastically informed him. "I been in de game fer goin' on twenty years, an' I never seen nobody dat packed de punch dat yuh do—*believe* me! Just lemme take yuh in hand, an' I'll make de greatest scrapper out uh yuh dat de woild has ever knew. Yuh train just de way I tell yuh, see? An' dere won't be nobody in de game dat can trim yuh."

But Charlie Chaplin introduced some training methods that were new, to say the least, during the days that followed.

The manager and chief handler of the ex-champion, Spike Dugan, who had transferred his allegiance to Charlie, had arranged a fight for him with Fluke McGlook, the runner-up to the welterweight championship. The way Charlie got into condition for it was this:

He rose at noon each day, and consumed one box of cigarettes before he had his breakfast. Then, entering with a gallon jug of beer in one hand, in the other he took a dumb-bell—not a pair of them, but one—and lifted it two or three times on a level with his chin. After which unviolent exertion, he fortified himself with a pull at the jug, and wandered over to the punching bag.

Charlie was delighted with this contrivance—at first. Here was something he could hit, and that wouldn't hit back. Charlie hit the bag. The bag swung back and hit him. Charlie hit it again, harder. The bag retaliated on the end of his nose.

Tipping his battered derby—which Charlie still wore, despite the fact that the rest of his costume was made up of a jersey and a pair of boxing trunks—to the bag, he walked away on his heels toward the yard of the training camp to do a little running.

Charlie crouching on his toes, with that dilapidated derby on his head, and with his mustache slanted at an angle of forty-five degrees as in strained attention he waited for the trainer behind him to fire his pistol into the air which would be the signal for him to go, made a laughable picture.

But he looked twice as funny when, the starting shot having been fired, he went galloping around the yard on his heels, with his arms sawing the air and his tongue hanging out—traveling, despite his desperate efforts, at the rate of about a hundred yards a minute.

It was after one such day's training, the news of Charlie's quick triumph over Spike Dugan, the erstwhile holder of the championship, having leaked out, as well as the fact that he was carded to fight Fluke McGlook before one of the local athletic clubs in a fortnight, that Charlie received a call from a tall, black-mustached stranger, who bore all the outward appearances of being a member of the gambling fraternity.

"Can I have a word with you?" the stranger asked confidentially of Charlie, coming up to him in the middle of the gymnasium floor where he stood looking speculatively at the punching bag.

"A word with me?" said Charlie pleasantly. "Yes, you can have—just one. You say 'Shake,' and I'll say 'No,' and then you can turn around and get out of here. For, without meaning any offense, I don't like your looks, and I wouldn't trust you any farther than I can throw you."

But the black-mustached stranger refused to take the none-too-gentle hint which Charlie had conveyed to him that his space in the gymnasium was desired more than his presence there.

Taking Charlie cordially by the arm, he led him off to one side.

"I want you to throw this fight," the stranger whispered in Charlie's ear. "If I can be sure you're going to lose, I can make a fortune by betting on McGlook—and out of what I'll clean up, I'm willing to do the fair thing by you."

Charlie looked at him, in sorrowing wonder.

"My dear fellow," he said kindly, "if you can find anybody in this city who's crazy enough to bet on my chances of winning this fight, take their money by all means—as much as you can get of it. You're bound to win. For I feel it in my bones that I am going to lose. I can't account for it, but that's the feeling I have."

The fact of the matter was, that Charlie had learned that it was against the Marquis of Queensbury rules to bring a horseshoe in a glove into the roped arena; and that was why he had such a strange feeling that he was not going to be returned the winner of the coming fight. But he meant to try his best to do so, nevertheless. In the first place, the winner's end of the purse would be larger than the loser's. But, also, there was the fairness of the thing to be considered—to give the people who might bet on him a "run for their money," in the parlance of the ring.

"You will have your little joke!" laughed the black-mustached stranger diplomatically. "But there's no chance of your losing—unless you try. The man who licked Spike Dugan in one punch—why, the fight's already as good as in. Fluke McGlook don't stand a chance against you, if you really start out to flatten him. But—I'm willing to pay you well for laying down to him. How much will you throw the fight for?"

Charlie shook his head, still good-humoredly.

"It can't be done," he replied.

Whereupon the gambler produced a revolver and pushed it into Charlie Chaplin's face. They were standing beside the shower in that corner of the gymnasium at the moment.

"I guess you'll agree to throw the fight," growled the stranger—"now!"

Charlie turned the handle that operated the shower beside him.

"Guess again," said he.

The water poured down upon the gambler, who had been standing directly under the shower while Charlie was just out of range of it; and, drenched and sputtering for breath, the black-mustached stranger turned and fled.

And then came the night of the great fight. The first round, between Fluke McGlook and the "Jersey Mosquito," as the referee had introduced Charlie Chaplin to the crowd at the ringside, damaged neither of the contestants. The reason for this being the fact that each had been unable to hit the other, try as they would. Their aim was bad.

The second round was more "lively," from the spectators' point of view. McGlook backed Charlie into a corner, and began to pommel him. Charlie was on the floor when the bell rang—it was all that saved him from a knock-out.

In the third, McGlook was weak from the blows he had expended on Charlie's anatomy; therefore, it was Charlie who backed his adversary into a corner and punched away at him throughout the round.

The fourth round opened with Charlie and McGlook each taking a mighty swing at each other, and both falling down. They were too weak to get up. The referee and the seconds of both set them on their feet again facing each other. Charlie fell forward into McGlook's arms, his mustache drooping down dejectedly. And McGlook hit him. He hit him again. A third time and a fourth time. And then——

There was a rush of something brown and white through the air. And Charlie Chaplin's faithful bulldog, entering the ring in his master's defense, took a death grip on the seat of McGlook's fighting trunks. Then Charlie began to pommel him in turn. McGlook, running around the ring in a vain effort to shake off the dog, who was helping Charlie defeat him, tripped and went down. Charlie sat on him while the referee counted him out.

And, amid the wild shouting and hysterical laughter of the crowd, Charlie Chaplin was champion.

His New Job

CHARLIE CHAPLIN walked into the office of a moving-picture concern. And the first thing his eyes lighted on was a pretty girl. She was sitting on one of the chairs outside the manager's door; waiting her turn, apparently, to apply for a position as a moving-picture actress. Charlie walked over to her, on his heels, and with his little cane under his arm. He tipped his hat. The girl looked up at him, with her brows lifted and the corners of her mouth drawn down, as if to discourage such familiarity in a stranger. And then Charlie Chaplin smiled. It did the trick! For who could resist that smile of whole-souled good-fellowship? The pretty girl smiled back, and Charlie Chaplin sat down beside her.

And then she burst out laughing. For, pressing down the brim of his derby hat with both hands, Charlie had released it, to let it fly straight up from his head—this, in belated recognition of the clerk who sat frowning at him at the desk, by which Charlie Chaplin had walked without the formality of presenting his card.

Turning to the girl beside him, Charlie's laugh rang out with hers. He pushed the end of his cane against her ribs. Then he apologized by raising his hat. And then he began to talk.

"What happened," he asked, "when all the matches struck in the East Side factory?"

"Why——" she began in surprise.

"The proprietor said, 'For dot you shall sulphur.' When is a gate not a gate? When it's a-swing—that was an easy one. But what is it that walks everywhere on its head?"

"I don't know," she giggled.

"The nail in the heel of your shoe. Caught you that time!" and Charlie Chaplin was about to give her another playful dig with his cane, but he remembered himself in time. He raised its crook handle to the back of the brim of his hat and tipped the battered derby to her instead.

"You're quite a comedian, aren't you?" laughed the girl.

"Hist!" Charlie caught her wrist, drawing down his brows and shifting his little black mustache fiercely from side to side as he leaned toward her. "The old mill, at midnight! Have the papers with you, or I swear that Lord Helpus shall know all—you hear me, girl? All! The gypsy's secret was not lost with her death. I, Humphrey Opdyke, know the truth. You are in meh power—har! har! har!"

His expression of mock ferocity lifting from his face, Charlie leaned back to smile reassuringly at her.

"You're a tragedian, too!" she exclaimed in admiring awe. "My, but you're versatile! Did you come here to see if you could get an opening to playing the villains in the pictures?"

"No," said Charlie Chaplin, shaking his head, while a noble, an inspired, look overspread his countenance; "no. I want to play the part for which I feel that I was intended at birth. The hero—ah, that is the role for me! I will show you that I know how to play one. Ah, Gwendolyn—or whatever your name may be—fly with me!" He had seized her hand again, this time in both of his, to fold it to his vest, on the wrong side, but he quickly righted the mistake. "Let us leave this place, and go hunt up a soda-water fountain. I will buy you all the strawberry sundaes that ten cents will pay for. Come where the sirup is thick and they give the most ice cream——"

"You'll have to excuse me," interrupted the girl, rising. "The manager isn't busy now, and I can go in and tell him how much I want to be a moving-picture actress—though I never have acted before. Wish me luck!"

Charlie Chaplin looked after her as she walked toward the door of the manager's office.

"I wish you luck," he murmured obediently—"and I'll have a little of the same."

The outer door opened, and a man came in. He was tall and thin, with a ruddy complexion and a bushy, blond mustache, and his two front teeth protruded. A piece of bark between them, and he would have looked like a beaver bringing home wood for the dam. He was a would-be moving-picture actor, too, it seemed; for he came over and sat down in the seat beside Charlie Chaplin. With the girl's departure, Charlie had moved into her chair, nearest the door, for it was his turn to go into the manager's office next.

"My word, but the day makes one languid!" murmured the arrival in an accent seldom heard off Piccadilly. "A bit of a snooze is in order. Right-o!"

Stifling a yawn, he slid to a half-recumbent posture in the chair. And then he draped one foot carelessly across Charlie Chaplin's lap. Charlie shoved it off. The man put it back again. Charlie threw it off once more, this time with such force that the Englishman, rousing, sat bolt upright in the chair and turned to look at him.

"Thanks, but I already have a valise," said Charlie Chaplin politely. Then, looking down at the other's feet, he corrected himself in a tone of surprise: "Oh, that's your foot!"

The man had taken out a cigarette and placed it between his lips. Now, while he groped for a match in his pocket, he thrust his face into Charlie's to glower at him. Charlie frowned back at him just as fiercely, bringing his face closer to the other's. And, seizing the end of the cigarette between his teeth, he drew back suddenly—thus depriving the Britisher of his contemplated smoke. Charlie lighted the cigarette instead, and blew a tantalizing cloud of the smoke under the other's nose.

"Look hyar!" expostulated the Englishman. "What is a bounder like you doing in a place of this sort?"

"I'm going in to see the manager," explained Charlie Chaplin, "as soon as he's disengaged."

"I jolly well think you'll wait for me," said the other stiffly.

"You're right, you're jollying yourself when you think that," responded Charlie, with cheerful firmness. "My turn comes next."

As he spoke, the door marked "Manager" opened, and the pretty girl with whom Charlie had chatted came out. He rose, raising his hat to her. Simultaneously, the outer door opened, and a long-haired, typical actor of the "old school" entered. Charlie Chaplin, exchanging a smile with the girl, who looked back over her shoulder at him as she passed out, did not see the newcomer stalk majestically toward the swinging door of the manager's office and pass through it—thus depriving him of his turn.

But the Englishman had witnessed it. He gave Charlie an impatient shove, as he stood bowing and scraping to the girl, and tried to run by him to forestall the aged tragedian's entrance to the private office.

"No, you don't!" cried Charlie Chaplin, thinking he was the one the other wanted to beat to the door, and running toward it ahead of him.

The door, through which the veteran Thespian had passed, swung back and hit him. He fell against the Britisher, who had followed at his heels, and they both sprawled on the floor. "You won't get there first!" shouted Charlie. "You're bally wrong—I will!" shrilled his rival. The private office beyond the door was in pandemonium. In thunderous tones, the actor who had gained access to the manager, and begun demonstrating his ability, was declaiming: "To be or not to be? That is the question!" While over and over the manager's voice, lifted in a vain effort to drown the tragedian's, was repeating, "Get out! Get out!" Charlie Chaplin picked himself up and again started for the door. The Englishman came after him.

And through the door, which suddenly flew open, the old-school actor came sailing. He landed on Charlie and caromed to the floor on all fours. Charlie Chaplin went back once more against the Britisher, and a second time they both lost their balance.

When Charlie got to his feet, the "ham actor" had gone. On his way to the door, Charlie spied a coin on the floor—it was a dime that had been shaken out of the Thespian's pocket by his violent dismissal from the manager's presence. Charlie bent over to pick it up.

"And ten makes twenty," said he.

The Englishman "leap-frogged" over his back and took hold of the handle of the manager's door.

Charlie Chaplin caught one of his feet and pulled him back. The man fell to kicking to free his imprisoned foot, and Charlie, stooping down, set his teeth in his ankle.

With a moan of pain, his persistent rival subsided on the floor, and Charlie walked across his prostrate form and into the manager's office.

The latter was a short, middle-aged, bushy-haired man. He paid no attention to Charlie Chaplin, as he stood beside his desk. Charlie coughed, to attract his notice. Still the manager went on writing furiously in an engagement book, without looking up. Charlie Chaplin reached across the desk and took the man's head in his hand, turning it around in his direction.

"I'm a surprise for you," he said, with his winning smile.

The manager picked up a long, black rubber speaking-tube, put one end of it to his ear, and presented the other to Charlie in significant silence.

"Schuyler 00419," Charlie Chaplin called absent-mindedly into the contrivance. Then, realizing his blunder, he wriggled his shoulders in confusion over his own stupidity. "This isn't a party wire, is it?" he spoke into the mouthpiece of the tube, endeavoring to make amends for the slip by treating it jocularly. "Nobody else can hear what I say to you, can they?"

The manager's face, as he held the receiving end of the tube to his ear, bore the same stony expression. Evidently he himself had not heard what Charlie said. The young man blew into the tube to attract his attention, as though it had been a dumb-waiter whistle. The manager lowered the apparatus and looked up at him, with the same blank expression.

"I can't hear you," he commented. "The thing must be stopped up."

"I'll fix it!" hastily offered Charlie Chaplin, eager to be of service to the man of whom he expected to ask a favor. "This ought to clear it out!" As he spoke, he picked up the inkwell, the first thing on which his eyes had chanced to light, and poured its contents into his end of the tube.

"I'll blow through it," said the manager, who had not heard what he said nor watched what he had done.

Charlie put his eye to his end to witness the possible removal of the obstruction in the tube that might result from the manager's promised experiment. The latter blew, as he said he would. And Charlie Chaplin received about two fluid ounces of ink in the face.

"Don't apologize!" he reassured the manager, as the latter attempted to do so. "It's the first painless black eye I ever got!"

The door opened. A tall, stately, gorgeously attired young woman came in. Two sandwich men, one preceding and the other following her, could not have heralded more plainly than her bearing did the fact that she was a "leading lady." Charlie Chaplin, flashing her his ever-ready smile, tipped his hat to her. She paid as much attention to his presence in the room as though he had been a hole in the atmosphere. The manager, who had turned back to the engagement book on his desk, was unaware of her arrival. Charlie picked up the tube, the other end of which the manager still held to his ear, and blew a tremendous whistle into it to notify him that she was there.

And then he wandered out of the office.

The Englishman, outside, was just coming to from the bite on his ankle. Charlie slapped him on the head with his foot, making him lie down again, and walked over his body once more.

Out onto the studio floor Charlie Chaplin sauntered, and into a scene that was being taken.

"Get out of here!" the director roared at him, stopping the camera. "What do you mean by butting in here like this and spoiling my scene?"

Charlie tipped his hat to him.

"I've come here to work as an actor," he explained. "Do you happen to need a hero?"

The busy director, thinking Charlie meant that the manager had engaged him, told him to go back to the latter's office and get a part. Charlie Chaplin, returning to the manager's room, picked up from the desk the thickest part in the pile he found there. If size counted for anything, he told himself, he had the leading part in his hand. He went back to the studio and up to the director.

"Do you know what this is, you chump?" the director demanded, after a glance at the twenty-odd typewritten pages Charlie had handed to him. "Look! It has written on it, plainly enough for you to see: 'Property Part; A King's Ransom.' That's where you belong, I guess, at that—the property room. Go in there and tell the carpenter to give you a plank, and bring it back here, in a hurry."

Charlie Chaplin picked up a board in the property room, without asking the permission of the carpenter, whose back was momentarily turned.

"Hey!" the carpenter called after him. Charlie turned around, and knocked him down with one end of the plank. Then he turned again to continue on his way, and the other end of the board which protruded from under his arm knocked down the Englishman, who had followed him to the property room.

"Pardon me, Matt!" Charlie Chaplin murmured, as he walked over the latter once more. "You don't mind my calling you Matt, do you, old rug?" And he passed on into the studio.

"Now, go back and get me another side for this set," the director ordered.

Charlie dropped the plank on the director's toes, and waddled away on his heels. He removed his coat, and swung it around and around in preparation to cast it aside. When the garment left his hand, it struck the Englishman, causing him to fall back against the carpenter, as they were both starting out of the property room to look for Charlie Chaplin. They went down in a heap. Charlie seized the piece of upright scenery the director had sent him after, and returned to the studio with it.

There, the first person he saw was the pretty girl with whom he had struck up an acquaintance in the office. Resting the piece of scenery against the director, Charlie leaned on it and began to hold a conversation with her.

"So the manager gave you a job, did he?" he greeted her.

Taking out a cigarette, he lit it—being careful to blow the smoke away from her. But unwittingly he blew it into the face of the leading lady, who was standing on his opposite side. Looking disdainfully down at him, she began to stiffen with indignation.

"I see the manager hired you, too," the pretty girl returned, regarding Charlie Chaplin's shirt-sleeved appearance in surprise. "But you don't look much like a hero in a play."

"Ah," Charlie explained, with a smile and an airily reassuring wave of his hand, "I am only waiting for my chance. That is the way for any one to succeed in the movies. Just wait around until the chance comes to break through——"

He staggered off his balance. He had broken through the canvas side of the piece of scenery against which he was leaning, as he spoke. He collided with the director, who in turn bumped into the leading lady, almost causing her to fall. She turned on the director, leveling an indignant finger at Charlie.

"Put that person out!" she ordered.

"I don't need to try *her* on a daisy," Charlie murmured to himself, as he moved away to stand looking on outside the studio set. "She loves me not!"

The director was having trouble with one of the "extra" men in the scene. It represented, he had explained to the performers, the queen's dressing room in the palace, on the eve of a grand ball.

The villain, a colonel of the Palace Guards, was to enter in haste, to inform her majesty that her royal spouse was impatiently awaiting her presence in the ballroom. The hero, a member of the colonel's regiment, the man she really loved, was with her. The extra man was playing the hero's part. The leading man having not yet arrived, it was necessary to have some one take his place for the rehearsal. The colonel, who suspected the love of the queen and the soldier, and who had determined to break off the affair, was to read him an order to ride forth on a dangerous mission that same night.

Twice the director had explained how the hero's leave-taking of the queen was to be acted, and twice the extra man had done it wrong. In desperation, the director looked around him, and his eye lighted on Charlie Chaplin.

"Here, you!" he ordered Charlie. "Go to the dressing room and get into a uniform, and come back here and see if you can play this part."

Charlie went off obediently. He came to the leading man's dressing room, and hesitated for a moment before the door at sight of the star it bore. Then he shrugged his shoulders, and went inside. Five minutes later, he had put on the leading man's uniform, his sword, and fur hat.

The things were much too big for him—especially the shako, which came down so far on his head as almost to cover his eyes. But he drew on the star's gloves, the fingers of which flapped emptily for a full inch, and went back to the director, with the sword clanking along the floor behind him.

On the way, Charlie Chaplin found the carpenter shooting craps all alone on the floor of the property room, for "mind bets" with himself.

"I shoot a dime," said Charlie Chaplin, laying the coin down on the floor as he spoke. "Give me those bones!"

As he shook them, the carpenter sawed the air with his hand, crouching over the money. And as Charlie rolled the dice out the carpenter snatched the coins up. The dice had not yet stopped rolling, so that their numbers could be read, and the fact of whether Charlie had lost or not ascertained. A bewildered expression on his face, Charlie started to protest.

"You lost, you lost!" the carpenter told him. "Roll again."

Charlie Chaplin laid down his last ten cents. Again, as he shook his dice, the carpenter's hand sawed the air above the money, like a referee's as he "counts out" a vanquished fighter. And again, as Charlie Chaplin made the motion to roll the dice out, the carpenter swept up Charlie's dime, and the one he had bet against it, from the floor.

"Say, what——" began Charlie, the bewildered look returning to his face.

"You lost, you lost!" repeated the carpenter.

Charlie opened his hand and showed him the dice in it.

"I haven't rolled them yet," he pointed out. "Now, put down that money!"

Sheepishly, the carpenter did so. Charlie picked up both dimes, the amount with which he had come into the game, and handed the dice back to the other.

"Come on, shoot again!" urged the carpenter. "I love to gamble."

"You mean," Charlie Chaplin corrected, shaking his head in refusal of the man's invitation, "you love to take candy away from little children, or rob blind beggars of the money in their tin cups. But I've had enough, thanks. If I stuck around with you long enough, I'd go walking out of here in a barrel."

He continued on his way to the director on the studio floor.

"Now," said the director, "you and the leading lady walk in together. Try it!"

They did—four times in all. Toward the end, the director very nearly had apoplexy. Charlie's walk was a thing no other human being could keep step with. And his entrance of the scene with the leading lady on his arm was anything but the poetry of motion.

"Come on!" the director called to the villain to enter the scene.

"Why don't you salute him?" the director shouted at Charlie through his megaphone. "He's your superior officer. Salute him with your sword!"

Charlie drew the weapon, and presented the hilt to his lips. Then he tried to put it back in the scabbard. It persistently resisted his efforts to fit it into the opening of the sheath.

"Somebody's been rubbing butter on it!" Charlie protested to the director.

"Go on, go on!" the latter called to the actor who was playing the part of the colonel of the Palace Guards. "Take out the order for him to ride into the next kingdom. Never mind reading all of it. Finish with, 'And if you refuse to undertake the mission, you will be shot at sunrise, as a traitor to your country.' "

Charlie fell on his knees and lifted his clasped hands toward the villain. He thought the piece of acting was what the situation demanded. The director held a different opinion.

"Don't take it like that!" the director raged at him. "You're not a coward, man—you're the hero of the play. Act more like one. Be calm. Now," to the colonel, "read it to him again."

" 'And,' the actor obeyed, 'if you refuse to undertake the mission, you will be shot at sunrise.' "

Charlie lifted his shoulders, and brought his hands down to his sides in a highly indifferent gesture.

"Well, whatever's the rule!' he remarked.

The director tore his hair.

"No, no, no!" he bellowed. "Nothing like it at all! Is that the way you'd hear an order that threatened you with death? Take it seriously—seriously, but nonchalantly."

"Oh!" said Charlie, in the tone of one on whom a great light has dawned. "Nonchalantly! Of course—why didn't you say so before? Try me again; I know what you want now."

As the actor spoke the line to him once more, Charlie Chaplin summoned a look of pained amazement to his face—the expression that would have been registered there, say, if he had unexpectedly been kicked by a mule. And then, with a snap of his fingers, he crossed his feet and put out his hand to lean against the pillar beside him. The pillar slipped from its base, and Charlie almost fell on his nose. He clutched the pillar in both arms, attempting to replace it, and it left the pedestal altogether. He staggered forward, he staggered back, and then he lost his footing, and fell with the pillar on top of him.

"And you said," the director addressed him scornfully, when the pillar had been lifted from his neck and replaced on its base, and Charlie Chaplin dragged to his feet, somewhat dazed, but unhurt, "you said you had come here to work as a hero! *Some* hero you are! But I'll give you another chance. You're going to ride on this mission. Lead the queen to the stairway, and take your leave of her."

Charlie pulled down the coat of his uniform, and offered the leading lady his arm. And, turning his back on the camera, he started with her toward the staircase that had been built at the rear of the studio setting, waddling slowly on his heels.

In the meantime, the leading man had arrived at the studio. He had hunted high and low in his dressing room for his uniform, sword, and hat. Failing to find them anywhere, he had rushed forth toward the studio floor in a towering rage.

At that moment, Charlie Chaplin had reached the stairway with the leading lady. She mounted a step, and he fell on his knees at her feet. Lifting the hem of her skirt to his lips, he pressed it there. Then he dried his imaginary tears, at their parting, from his eyes, on it. She mounted another step. Charlie held on to her train, ardently kissing it again. There was a ripping sound, but he was carried away by the emotion he fondly hoped he was registering at their separation, and he gave no heed to it. In blissful ignorance, also, of what had happened, the leading lady went on up the stairway—in a skirt which ended halfway to her knees, and whose train remained tightly clutched in Charlie Chaplin's hands.

The director, seizing him by the collar, dragged him to his feet.

"You're fired!" he roared. "It's a lucky thing for you there's a law in the land—or you'd be killed! Get out of here!"

He aimed a blow at Charlie's head as he spoke. The leading man came running up to find out who had stolen his costume, at that moment. Charlie ducked. And the star got the blow, instead.

Charlie Chaplin ran in the only direction that was open—the property room. He met the Englishman with the bushy, blond mustache and the prominent front teeth, coming out of it. He took a punch at Charlie. And again Charlie ducked. The blow hit the director, who had run after him. The carpenter rose in Charlie's path, and swung for his head. Ducking once more, Charlie allowed the punch to swing harmlessly over his head and meet the leading man, who had pursued the director. Running out of the property room, Charlie looked back through its door. The Englishman and the director, the star and the carpenter were all rolling about the floor, pommeling each other.

"You can fight it out among yourselves!" Charlie whispered, with a smile, turning away. "May the best man win! I'm going to get out of this costume, and see if I can find that pretty girl. And some soda-water counter is going to be twenty cents richer!"

By the Sea

CHARLIE CHAPLIN came down the board walk, eating a banana. The direction in which he was heading was north. And one of his feet, in their battered "number thirteens," was pointed to the east while the other was aimed due west, so that as he walked straight ahead he had to propel himself entirely by his heels.

He took a bite of the banana. Then, forgetting that he had just done so, he took another bite. The result was a collision between both mouthfuls. One of them had to go. It did.

Charlie looked down at the yellow skin in his hand, to find that it was empty. His absent-mindedness had caused him to lose at least a third of the banana—the amount of his second mouthful, which he had not been able to manage, and that had rolled through a crack in the board walk at his feet out of sight.

His expression grew sad. He twirled his little bamboo cane, and turned his head to the right and then to the left. Then, dropping the banana skin on the walk, he started forward once more, and slipped on the peel and fell down.

His expression was sadder than ever when he picked himself up.

Advancing another hundred feet along the board walk, Charlie Chaplin stopped beside a man who was absorbed in watching his own feet. They were behaving in a strange way. If it had been ice, instead of a summer-resort board walk on which he stood, a beholder would have said that he was engaged in executing the fancy skater's feat of "cutting the figure eight."

The man had been drinking—something a great deal stronger than lemonade.

On the stiff wind that was blowing, Charlie got a whiff of alcohol from his direction. He clapped his hand to his brow, staggering. Then another gust of wind cleared his reeling senses, and he started to walk rapidly away from the convivial party's dangerous proximity.

As he did so, the wind blew his derby off. It swept the tipsy individual's straw hat from his head at the same moment. Both headpieces shot out at the end of the "trolleys" fastened in their owners' buttonholes, and the two strings wound around each other.

"Excuse me!" said Charlie Chaplin, flashing his white teeth in an apologetic smile at the unsteady stranger, and pulling his derby out of the air to clap it back on his bushy hair.

"Scush me!" thickly echoed the "souse," recovering his own hat and replacing it on his head likewise.

And then they both started off in opposite directions.

Their trolleys being still tangled, the hat of each was jerked off his head again as they moved apart.

Both swung around to face each other, tethered by the cords at their buttonholes like a pair of spaniels out for an airing on a double leash.

"Excuse me!" repeated Charlie Chaplin. And "Scush—hic—me!" said the pifflicated individual again.

They made a simultaneous grab for their hats once more, and each one got the other's by mistake and put it on his head. They started to walk away again.

Off went their hats a second time, their trolleys now tangled more hopelessly than ever.

"Say, look here——" began Charlie impatiently.

The other walked unsteadily up to him to thrust his face into his.

"Wassaidearhuh?" he said.

Charlie Chaplin regarded him puzzledly.

"Oh—pleased to meet you!" He misunderstood the man's jumbled words. "But, now, Wassie, old top—you don't mind my calling you Wassie, do you?—if you'll give me back my hat, I'll be moving along."

"Wassa—idear—huh?" repeated the befuddled stranger, spacing the words by pushing his forefinger into Charlie Chaplin's chest after each one. His eyebrows worked menacingly up and down as he continued to hold Charlie's gaze with his own, his nose not an inch away from his face. "Tryin' to get gay with me? Huh? That it? Huh? Punch your head off."

Backing away as the man talked, Charlie had brought him after him—as the magnet draws the steel—by the trolley that was tangled up with his.

Suddenly he fell over backward off the board walk. The pickled party shot through the air after him at the end of the string, to land on top of him on the sand below.

"Shay—hic—this's *stoo* much!" the man declared, scrambling up and starting belligerently toward Charlie, who had also regained his feet. "I'm goin' push your face inter th' middle next week—fresh guy!"

Charlie lifted his foot, as the other came for him, and sent him spinning back off his balance with a shove of its broad, flappy sole.

But he forgot that he was still attached to him—married, as it were, by the circumstance of the twisted trolleys that bound him to him. "Whither thou goest, there will I go," says the poet, referring to the duty of those joined in holy wedlock. The stewed party went backward, head over heels, to land on all fours on the beach once more, and Charlie Chaplin went with him—like a big fish jerked out of the water at the end of the black cord that fastened him to the other.

As they rose, the overtaxed trolleys snapped, and each was now free to go his own way. Charlie started to take advantage of that fact.

But the man with the "package" was bent on following up his threat to fight him, it seemed.

Charlie tried to calm him by tipping his hat rapidly at him two or three times by the back of the brim, with a smile of appealing good-fellowship.

But still the man came weaving his way deliberately toward him, with his doubled fists revolving slowly around each other, as though he was rolling up an invisible ball of twine.

Charlie Chaplin's face became woebegone.

He glanced uneasily out of the corner of his eye at the menacing approach of his would-be antagonist. Twirling his cane, he shifted his weight from foot to foot.

He did not want to fight. It was the truth, to which he could have sworn on a stack of Bibles three feet high—he did *not* want to fight. When a boy, he had made a promise at his mother's knee that he would never engage in anything of that coarsening sort. And you know how one feels about breaking such a vow. But it wasn't that he was afraid.

Charlie's shoulders shrugged nervously up and down, as the man came to a halt before him. The stewed party took his face in both hands, and tilted it to just the angle he desired.

And then Charlie, fastening his eyes at a spot on the sand, began to bend forward, as though to obtain a closer view of some treasure his gaze had lighted on there. The man, turning unsteadily to line up beside him, began to stoop over, too, to see what he was looking at.

When he had bent down far enough to suit him, Charlie straightened at his side and wrapped his arm around his neck in a tight embrace. And then he brought up his other hand and punched him in the nose.

The man made a moaning sound, like a dog who wants to get in the house on a rainy night, and sagged limply down in Charlie's arm.

He hit him again. It was a beautiful day. The yellow beach that shelved down to the white surf which separated the turquoise blue of the ocean beyond, made the view a pleasure to the eye. He uppercut the souse again. Ah, yes, Charlie Chaplin told himself, the seashore on a cloudless day in July like this was the place to be.

And then he let go of the man, who slipped forward, to stand on his head and feet on the sand, like an inverted V, as he caught sight of something else which verified his impression that he had been wise in coming to that summer resort to spend a holiday.

It was a girl, on whom his serenely roving gaze had just rested. She was a peach! And she was coming that way. Charlie straightened his frayed necktie, smoothed back his hair at either side of his forehead, and put on his most winning smile.

"Whither away, little one?" he inquired, as she passed.

The girl stopped to look him slowly up and down with a scornful glance.

"Aw, wither away yerself!" she said out of the side of her mouth, shifting the gum she was chewing to do so.

Charlie started, and his eyebrows lifted in distressed surprise at the rudeness of her speech. She was either a shopgirl, or she had once been one, who had come down to the beach for a day's outing. But she was pretty. There was no mistake about that. And Charlie smiled at her again.

"Oh, you little checkerboard!" he called roguishly, as she was walking off, referring to the black-and-white check suit she wore. "It's not your move—away from me, is it?"

The girl stopped.

"Say," she explained grimly, "I'm lookin' for my husband, and if he leans his bunch of fives up against your silly-lookin' face, *you'll* move over into the next county so fast you could give an aeroplane three miles head start and beat it out by a city block—see?"

Nothing daunted, Charlie took the handkerchief out of the souse's hip pocket, which was conveniently upturned beside him, as the latter continued to occupy the position of the ostrich who hides his head in the sand, and waved it after her.

She burst out laughing—she couldn't help it—and Charlie took it for an encouraging omen, and hastened after her on his heels.

"Charming day, isn't it?" he addressed her conversationally.

Her brows were drawn down once more

"Beat it!" she said.

Charlie, instead, secured her hand.

"This little pig went to market," he began lightly, picking up her fingers one at a time; "this little pig stayed home; this little pig——"

He was interrupted. The souse, who had "come to" and followed him for the purpose of continuing their dispute, tapped him on the shoulder.

Charlie, looking around to see who the intruder was, turned back to the girl and apologetically raised his hat to her. His foot shot out behind him, catching the tipsy man in his "lunch box," and sending him swishing back through the air to where he had come from.

The souse, bent double from the force and the location of Charlie's reverse-English kick, brought up with such a jarring thump against the wooden stand that held a life preserver suspended by a pair of pegs from its cross arms that the round buoy came down on him.

It fell around that portion of his anatomy which was uppermost as he stood leaning over, and held him in that position with the security that a barrel might if he had sat down in it.

"What were we saying?" Charlie Chaplin was resuming to the girl. "Oh, yes—you were telling me that you had never met a man who exerted my strange fascination over you. That if I should ask you to go up on the board walk with me and sit down on that bench up there, and tell you to put your arms around me and give me a kiss, you would be unable to resist the——"

He broke off once more. A dazed look spread over his face, as the life preserver, from which the souse had finally succeeded in extricating himself, struck him on the back of the head.

"Pardon me," he told her, tipping his hat. "There's a troublesome party over there who's my father's private secretary. My father, you know, is a millionaire. We're not on speaking terms. His secretary is trying to get me to come home, and he's desperate enough to be trying to knock me senseless, and then carry me there. Excuse me just a moment."

And, picking up the life preserver, he threw it back at the man.

"You a millionaire!" the girl laughed derisively. "You're a tramp, that's what you are! In them pants, that must have been handed down to you by President Taft when he got through at the White House, and that secondhand derby, and them busted-down canal boats on your feet, d'ye think anybody wouldn't know you for a panhandlin' hobo——"

"Then my disguise is perfect!" broke in Charlie, with unshaken good humor. "You will see why I am dressed this way, when I have told you the story of my life, as I mean to do up there on that bench——"

But at that moment he was unexpectedly called away from her side.

There was no time for him to resist the summons, for it was conveyed in the form of the life buoy with which the souse had lassoed him, jerking him off the sand and through the air like a shot out of a gun, to hale him back to the scene of their argument.

Picking himself up, Charlie threw off the life preserver and walked up to his persistent challenger, his lips pressed together in a thin line, which showed that he had reached the end of his patience.

The souse was teetering forward on his toes and then back on his heels, his arms swaying loosely from his bent-over shoulders.

Charlie planted himself in front of him, and began to swing his arm around in the air.

"One, two, three, four," he counted its revolutions, and when he had got up to "twenty-three" he let the blow go.

The inebriated party performed the difficult acrobatic feat of making a complete double somersault in the air, and fell over on his back on the sand for the full count.

But the girl, when Charlie Chaplin returned to the spot where he had left her, was gone.

He shrugged his shoulders, and twirled his little bamboo cane, to try to get over the disappointment. Then, shuffling across the sand, he mounted to the board walk again and started along it. A smile broke over his visage the next moment. Hobbling quickly forward, more on one leg than on the other, he approached the girl he had lost on the bench, and whom he had just spied sitting alone on a bench ahead of him.

"Why, how do you do?" she said cordially.

There should have been something in the change in her manner toward him, as she moved over, with a welcoming smile, to afford him a seat on the bench beside her, to warn Charlie that all was not going to be well with him if he accepted her mute invitation.

But he did not notice it, or the look she threw over her shoulder in the direction of a cigar stand behind them, either.

"You're a terror with the girls, ain't you?" she went on, with a smile of mock reproof, as he seated himself beside her.

"Oh, well," Charlie Chaplin protested, looking down at the tip of one shoe and turning his head from side to side as he smote it with his cane, "I don't like to talk about myself, you know!"

The girl's eyes came back to him from another furtive look toward the cigar stand.

"I've got your number, all right," she assured him. "Old Mr. George W. Ladykiller—that's you!"

Charlie sat up closer to her.

"Like me?" he questioned softly. So intent was he upon following up what seemed to be the "hit" he was making with the girl, that he did not see the tall, broad-shouldered man—her husband—who had returned from the cigar stand and now stood glowering down at him over the back of the bench. "Go on and like me, for I like—I like——"

Charlie stopped. He looked up slowly over his shoulder, and saw the man, who looked ferocious enough to eat him alive as he returned his innocent gaze with an angry glare. Charlie put up his hand and coughed weakly.

He seemed to find his collar too tight all at once, and the day warmer than was comfortable, for he tugged at his necktie with one hand and with the other pulled out his handkerchief and mopped his brow.

In ominous silence, the husband of the girl beside whom he sat came around the end of the bench and sat down on it with them.

His burly weight, descending on that end of the bench, caused the one on which Charlie Chaplin was seated to rise like a springboard. It shot him into the air, and away in the direction he wanted to go—which was as far from that bench as he could get.

Five minutes later, he halted before a soda-water booth.

And, as he did so, he wheeled at the sound of a familiar voice in his rear.

Charlie Chaplin groaned, for, confronting him, was the soused individual. The spirits he carried aboard, or a streak of obstinacy in his nature which he possessed normally, made the man bent on settling his fight with him. But it seemed he had undergone a change of heart toward Charlie.

"Le's call—hic—bygones, bygones," said he, holding out his hand. "You 'n' me'll be frien's—whatcha say?"

Charlie Chaplin gripped his hand dramatically.

"We are friends," he declaimed.

They turned away from each other. Then the souse spun around.

"Frien's!" he echoed Charlie's heroic tone, again holding out his hand.

Charlie took it, and clapped his other hand down on the wabbling one's shoulder. They looked, standing thus, like a travesty on a group statue labeled "Damon and Pythias."

"We ought to celebrate our friendship in some way," suggested Charlie, turning to the booth beside them. "Have something on me, won't you?"

They lined up at the counter together;

"Scotch high ball," he ordered.

"No, no! You're in the wrong place," Charlie Chaplin hastily corrected him. "Have an ice-cream cone. Go ahead, the novelty of it may make you like it."

The clerk gave them the two cones, filled with ice cream.

"Ten cents," he addressed Charlie.

"Not bad, are they?" Charlie, with his mouth full and ignoring the clerk, asked his companion. "Taken in moderation, and on a hot day, I always say——"

"Say," the clerk broke in sternly, "who's goin' to pay for them? I'm waitin' to get ten cents."

"All right," Charlie encouraged him. "Keep on waiting. A rich uncle may die and leave it to you some day."

"Don't get funny, young feller!" threatened the clerk. "Which one of youse is comin' across with the dime, now?"

"My friend will pay you," said Charlie.

"No, I won't!" denied the souse.

"Give him ten cents."

"Nossir. You asked me to have this on you——"

"But you're drunk and I'm sober. You don't suppose I'd buy one of these things in my right mind? It's going to be on you."

The intoxicated individual—but lately his sworn friend—scooped the ice cream out of his cone, and, his face red with rage, threw it at Charlie Chaplin's head.

Charlie ducked in time, and the moist gob met the husband of the girl he had lately been flirting with full in the face, as that burly personage stood at the cigar stand near by, where he had gone to purchase another smoke.

Charlie Chaplin dug the ice cream out of *his* cone and threw it at the souse. His aim was better than the latter's had been. The lump of frozen sweetness plastered his nose and mouth.

"I told you," said Charlie good-naturedly, "that it was going to be on you—and it is!"

The intoxicated stranger's eyes were blinded by the sticky mass. The burly man whose face had received the fistful of ice cream that was meant for Charlie came running up to them at that moment with a passing policeman, whom he had hailed. And the souse struck out at Charlie. He ducked again, and the cop received the blow in his stead.

"And I thought," said Charlie Chaplin dolefully, as he walked away from the turbulent scene, "that the seashore was a nice, pleasant, restful place to be!"

But again his spirits rose with a bound, as he caught sight of a second girl—and a pretty one, too—who was sitting on another bench on the board walk. Hastening eagerly up to her, Charlie sat down at her side.

Tss! tsst! His winning ways!

In five minutes, he had her first name, his arm around her waist, and her hand in his. *She* didn't care, it seemed, whether he looked like a tramp or not. And she wasn't married—at least, she didn't mention the fact.

Absorbed in his wooing of her, Charlie did not see the man with a prominent jaw and a checked cap pulled down to his eyes who came along and sat down in menacing silence on the end of the bench beside him.

But the girl did, and, with a startled gasp, she rose and fled. He was her husband. Charlie, his rapt gaze fixed straight before him at the moment, was unaware of her departure. Likewise, he did not perceive that the big, thickset husband of the girl he had first tried to flirt with had slipped into the second girl's place beside him.

The bench was rapidly filling up—with trouble.

The souse came up with a brick in his hand, and he, too, sat down quietly on the same bench. And at his heels was the cop, wearing the black eye he had received in the mix-up that had followed Charlie's refusal to pay for the ice-cream cones at the soda-water booth.

"Ah," said Charlie, turning as he did so toward the girl he thought he was addressing, "for a really good time, give me a day by the sea, with——"

He stopped. The burly man who sat in the girl's place was glowering at him. Beside him he saw the souse, with the brick poised and waiting in his hand. And behind *him* the policeman, with one eye swollen and closed and his lips determinedly set. Then he felt a nudge from his rear. Turning, he looked at the owner of the undershot jaw and the checked cap.

"Go ahead!" the husband of the girl with whom he had just been sitting on the bench grimly invited him to continue his remarks.

"No," faltered Charlie Chaplin, "I think I'll go—back!"

And he suited the action to the word, taking the only way out of the tight box in which he was cornered by throwing himself suddenly against the back of the bench, and it went over with all hands, except Charlie—who did a somersault, landing on his feet behind the sprawling others, and ran for it.

A Night Out

CHARLIE CHAPLIN had been looking on the wine when it was pink, violet, green, and yellow; in other words, he had just consumed sixteen poussé cafés.

It was a silly drink for him to pick out. That is to say, it would have been a silly drink for him to pick out if he had had anything to do with its selection. He had not done so, as a matter of fact. His lifelong pal—a man on whom he had never set eyes before that night, incidentally—had chosen the rainbow-hued and innocent-appearing, but highly explosive, drink for him. And Charlie, as he mounted the steps of the hotel, was—well, he was not what a truthful person could have called exactly sober.

His pal had preceded him fifteen minutes before to the room in that hotel which he and Charlie had engaged earlier in the evening; at least, he had said something about going there to "take forty winks before curfew rings, and the big time starts on Broadway."

But now, due to those sixteen multicolored drinks with which Charlie had surprised and temporarily stunned his stomach, Charlie forgot that he was stopping there—what, indeed, he had come into the place for at all.

Stopping at the desk, he groped vainly with his foot for a rail upon which to rest it.

The clerk who had given Charlie and his new-found friend their key had gone off duty since then. The proprietor of the hotel himself was in charge of the desk. Failing to find the rail for which he was seeking, Charlie found something else—the bottle of ink beside the open register—and he lifted it to his lips and was about to drain it.

"Here, here!" exclaimed the owner of the hotel, depriving him of the inkwell in the nick of time. "That's not to drink, you idiot; it's put there to sign your name with in this book; that is, if you want a room here."

Laughing pleasantly at his own mistake, Charlie murmured something to the effect that a room was one thing above all others he wanted just then. The proprietor handed him the pen, and Charlie dipped it in the ink and stirred it vigorously around.

Then, drawing the register toward him, he shook the surplus of ink from the pen—onto the hotel owner's shirt front.

The latter expostulated. But Charlie paid no heed to him. He was absorbed in a critical examination of the pen point. He wiped it off on the proprietor's beard. Again the latter started to protest. But once more Charlie ignored him. Dipping the pen into the ink a second time, his brows were knit in a frown of concentration as he began to inscribe his signature upon the page of the register before him.

Meanwhile, a heavily veiled girl or woman—the thickness of the veil prevented one from hazarding even a guess as to her age, or what her face was like—had entered the hotel lobby. She came to the pillar directly behind Charlie, and, propping one foot upon the leather seat around it, bent down to attend to a refractory shoe lace.

Charlie, in the physical and mental efforts he was making to sign his name, backed into her.

Looking around, with a start, he lifted his hat to the fair unknown and flashed her his friendly smile. Then, turning around to the register once more, he attempted to back into her again.

But the veiled object of his questionable attentions, having completed the retying of her shoe, was no longer there. Charlie sprawled on the floor of the lobby, bringing the hotel register with him. Lying there at full length, with the book open before him, Charlie mechanically finished writing his name in it, his eyes meanwhile following the lady whose unexpected removal of her presence from his immediate proximity had been responsible for his downfall, as she moved slowly across the lobby, looking back at him over her coyly shrugging shoulder.

Picking himself up, Charlie zigzagged, rather than walked, up to her. He raised his hat by the back of the brim.

"Won't you let a little sunshine filter into this dull place," he gallantly requested, "by raising your veil?"

She promptly obliged.

"O-o-h!" breathed Charlie, wincing as he looked on a long nose, a sallow complexion, two cross eyes, and a mouthful of gold teeth. Reaching up, he pulled the veil down over her face again as if it had been a shade. "Good *night!*"

Then, holding on to the sides of his derby with both hands, as though the sight of that ultrahomely countenance behind the veil had made not only his head but the hat above it ache, he turned sharply around and marched stiffly away on his heels.

Charlie found that his pal, whose acquaintance he had first made in the barroom where the poussé café had been introduced to Charlie's wondering, and at the same time protesting, digestive apparatus, was not in the hotel room.

His unexplained absence did not worry Charlie. The sight of the bed reminded him that he was very weary, and, despite the fact that it was still early in the evening, he prepared to retire.

With his coat off, Charlie went around looking for a place to hang it. He placed it on the wall where a hook should have been, and turned away. The garment dropped to the floor. Again, and yet again, Charlie, weaving his way unsteadily about the room, placed the coat upon the wall, only to have it fall in a heap at his feet. Finally, he thrust the coat unwittingly through the window, and when he let go of it it did not fall on the floor—but onto the sidewalk, three stories below.

Having thus satisfactorily—to him—got rid of the problem of where to hang that much of his clothing, Charlie did not invite a further one by seeking a place to hang up the rest of his garments, but let them lie scattered about the floor as fast as he took them off.

Only his little bamboo cane was he careful of. He put that in the bed, adjusting its handle tenderly on the pillow, and drew the sheet up over it.

Then in his pajamas, and with his toothbrush and a tube of dentifrice in his hands, he stepped into the bathroom adjoining.

Squeezing the tube of tooth paste above the toothbrush, Charlie sought to drop the long, serpentine coil of aromatic paste which the pressure of his fingers released from the mouth of the tube upon the surface of the brush. With his head bent over the task, and slowly teetering from his heels to his toes, and back to his heels again, paste and brush persistently missed connections. At last he was successful; the paste fell upon the bristles, and continued to fall upon them, until what looked like the filling of a charlotte russe was heaped upon the brush. But by that time Charlie had forgotten what he had brought the brush for. Lifting one foot to the edge of the white tile wash-stand, he proceeded to shine his shoe. And then, his eyes lifting to the shelf above, he noticed that the white paint in which it had originally been finished, to match the other fixtures in the bathroom, had become sadly chipped and worn away.

Lowering his foot, Charlie set to work, with all an artist's absorption in the task, to paint the edge of the shelf with the remainder of the tooth paste on his toothbrush.

It was just at this time that a man and his wife and their pet collie arrived at the hotel, unknown to Charlie Chaplin. They were assigned to a room on the third floor also, and directly across the hall from him. The husband—he was a powerfully built, black-browed individual, with an undershot, "fighting" jaw —went out, leaving his wife and the dog alone together in the room.

Donning a suit of pajamas, too, in preparation for retiring, she began to romp with the collie.

The dog, seizing one of her slippers, ran round and round the room, refusing to yield to her repeated, half-laughing commands that he drop the slipper. And then, before she could stop him, the collie bolted out of the room and ran into Charlie's across the hall.

The wife of the bull-necked and sour-visaged man went after the frolicsome canine. The dog had gone under Charlie's bed with the slipper. Dropping on her hands and knees, she crawled under after him. As she did so, the collie—still with the slipper between his grinning jaws—ran out and dashed back into the room across the hall from which he had come, and at the same moment Charlie Chaplin came back from the bathroom.

In his pajamas, and with his battered derby hat still perched on top of his bushy hair, Charlie sat down on the side of the bed and interestedly watched the room spinning round and round him.

He raised his hand weakly toward his brow; it paused six inches away from it.

Not hearing him stir, the wife of the thickset individual, who had been caught under Charlie's bed by his unexpected return to the room, had seized that moment to escape from her unhappy position. And Charlie, happening to glance down at that moment, had seen a woman's head protruding from beneath his bed.

Instantly, meeting his surprised gaze, she drew her head back out of sight.

Charlie stared about him bewilderedly.

"I could understand," he murmured, "my seeing two of us in the room. But one of us couldn't be a girl. Have I got 'em—or did I really see her head sticking out under the bed?"

Charlie swung his feet up onto the side of it, and sat there with his arms locked around his knees—waiting. He put out one hand, after a moment or so, and poked it inquiringly under the bed. Farther and farther under the bed he thrust his hand, and farther and farther off his balance he leaned on top of it. He toppled over on the floor on all fours, his derby rolling half under the bed.

And, looking beyond it, Charlie gazed into the angrily flushed face of the fair intruder upon the privacy of his bedroom.

Charlie waved a gay greeting to her.

"One, two, three for you!" said he. "I've found you, and now it's your turn to be It while I hide."

The girl scrambled out from under the bed, and, screening herself from Charlie's gaze with the two pillows from it, backed away from him.

"Go away!" she ordered him.

Charlie, sitting on the floor, looked up at her.

"Aren't you forgetting," said he, "whose room this is?"

"Go away!" repeated the girl.

"If I were in your room," Charlie pointed out to her, "you could order me to do so. But you're not in your room. As it happens, you're in mine. I could tell you to do the same thing—go away—if I wanted to. But I'm not sure that I do. I think I like to have you around."

The girl's husband, meanwhile, had come back to their room and found her gone from it. He went downstairs to the proprietor behind the desk, bawling his wife's name in no uncertain tones as he went, to demand of the owner of the hostelry immediate information as to the whereabouts of his spouse.

"I don't know where your wife is," the hotel proprietor told him.

The husband started wildly back upstairs again.

"She won't know where she is, either," he made the forbidding assertion, for her absence had angered him through and through, "when I get hold of her!"

In the hall outside the room in which his wife and Charlie Chaplin were confronting each other, the brawny man shouted her name again.

"Maria! Maria!"

Charlie, hearing the thunderous voice intoning that word over and over in the passageway without, looked inquiringly at the girl before him.

"Does your name happen to be Maria?" he inquired.

The girl answered grimly:

"It is. And that's my husband calling me."

Charlie turned and opened the door a crack. Through the crack he looked out into the hall. He caught a glimpse of the six-foot muscular man as he rushed by in search of his mysteriously strayed wife. Instantly Charlie closed the door again.

He leaned back against it, and from an upright posture slid down along its panels to a sitting one upon the floor.

"He," Charlie faltered to the girl, "he's a—a big man, isn't he?"

"He is," said the girl, through tight-pressed lips, still grimly.

"Don't you think you'd better go back," Charlie suggested, "to your own room?"

The girl laughed a short, bitter laugh of derision.

"And run smack into him?" she questioned. "No, I don't think I'd better do that—and it wouldn't be the best thing that could happen to you, either, if I was such a fool as to let him see me coming out of this door."

Charlie lifted himself slowly from the floor, and opened the door for an inch or so once more. Then he closed the door again, and turned to face the girl.

"The coast is clear!" he informed her.

It was the truth. Her husband had run downstairs again, having failed to find his wife in their room, to inquire a second time of the proprietor if he knew anything of her whereabouts.

"If he isn't in the hall," the girl suggested to Charlie, "he may be waiting for me in our room."

"No, for the door is standing open," Charlie reassured her on that point. "He must have gone downstairs. And now's your chance to skip back where you came from without a soul the wiser—if you're afraid to go alone, I'll go with you."

She drew herself up at the suggestion, born in his fuddled senses, and essayed to freeze him with a haughty stare.

"If you dare!" she threatened.

And, opening the door of Charlie Chaplin's room, and peering out into the hall to satisfy herself that the coast *was* clear, as he had said, she dashed back into the room from which she had come.

She gave an exasperated exclamation as she turned to close the door. Charlie Chaplin stood on the threshold of her room.

"I'm with you," he assured her, with a smile, "to the finish."

"Go back where you came from," she warned, "or, if my husband catches you here, it will mean *your* finish."

"You don't want me around?" asked Charlie, as though trying to get the matter straight in his mind.

"I certainly don't!" she replied emphatically.

"Don't want to tell me the story of your life and listen to mine?" went on Charlie.

"No!" said the girl.

"You don't like me at all, then?" Charlie asked her.

"Will—you—get—out—of—here?"

Charlie nodded gravely, and walked to the bed.

"Good night," he said politely.

And, sitting down on the side of the bed, he thrust his legs under the covers, laid his head on the pillow, and settled himself to go to sleep.

The wife of the stalwart man ran to him and shook his shoulder.

"Get up and go back to your own room!" she exclaimed. "If my husband should come back here, as he's likely to do any minute, and find you——" She broke off with a gasp of alarm.

From the hall outside rose the thunderous tones of her husband's voice once more, growing momentarily nearer.

"Maria! Maria!"

The girl looked from the door outside which her lord and master was roaring her name to Charlie Chaplin in the bed, and backed away, trembling.

"Oh, dear! Now you can't get out!"

The only answer she received was a gentle snore from the bed.

At that moment there was a pounding on the door. It announced the arrival outside it of her husband. The girl wrung her hands at the helplessness of her position. She could not wake Charlie Chaplin, who was slumbering as peacefully as a child in the bed. And if she did, how could she get him out of the room, with her husband standing in front of its door?

"Maria! Maria!" shouted the burly man.

Once more the pounding sounded on the door.

She did the only thing she could to get out of her dilemma, or to make an attempt to: Running to the bed, she pulled the sheet up over Charlie, thus concealing him from view. And then she went to the door, pausing to throw an apprehensive look over her shoulder at the mound under the sheet that marked where Charlie lay, and then opened the door.

With a face as black as a thundercloud, her husband strode into the room.

"Where have you been?" he demanded.

His wife backed away before his lowering gaze.

"Why—why——" she faltered.

"Speak up! Where were you?"

"Why, I—I'll tell you, Horace," she explained. "It—it's a long story."

"In that case," said her husband, with grim irony, "I'd better sit down to listen to it."

He crossed to the bed. And, seating himself upon it, he sat down on top of Charlie Chaplin's recumbent form under the sheet. Slowly, with his eyes fixed accusingly upon his wife, the powerfully built man rose. He turned and took hold of the top of the sheet between his finger and thumb, and pulled it back. Charlie lay revealed under it.

Opening one eye, Charlie inquired sleepily of nobody in particular:

"Is it seven o'clock yet?"

With a roar, whose duplication, once or twice every hour, would have drawn crowds flocking to a circus side show in which he was enacting the rôle of a Wild Man of Borneo, the girl's husband pulled Charlie out of the bed by the collar of his pajama coat.

"What d'ye mean?" he demanded of Charlie, holding him fiercely with his eye. "What're you doing in here? Answer me?"

Charlie smiled deprecatingly.

"I was sleeping," he answered, "when you woke me up."

The man, who was twice as big as he was, snorted in inarticulate rage.

"Why," said Charlie, looking around him in pretended surprise, "why—this isn't my room! I've made a mistake. I beg your pardon, I'm sure!"

He started to walk to the door. The thickset man aimed a blow at him, which Charlie ducked. In a bound, he reached the door and threw it open. Across the hall he ran toward his own door—with the burly individual after him.

The latter chased Charlie around the bed in the room from which he had wandered into the one across the hall, that was shared by the burly individual and his wife.

Charlie succeeded in dodging him, and ran out across the hall and into the other room again.

Here the girl's husband followed him, and chased him around the bed from which he had dragged Charlie. Back across the hall once more, and into his own room, Charlie ran. But he could not shake off his persistent pursuer. There was only one way that he could hope to do so. And that way Charlie took.

He dove, headfirst, out of his bedroom window.

Fortunately, a passer-by broke his fall on the sidewalk three stories below. It is a well-known fact that those under the influence of alcohol are strangely impervious to injury. That is why Charlie rose from his collision with the pedestrian on whose shoulders he had descended from the air, unharmed. And why, also, the person who had received his weight thus unexpectedly likewise scrambled up unhurt.

The person was his pal.

"I was just coming to look for you," the latter informed Charlie Chaplin, embracing him. "Come on; let's go get a drink."

Linking arms with the other, Charlie drew him toward the entrance of the hotel.

"Come up to the room with me while I get dressed," said he, "and then I'm with you. I need a drink— after what I've just gone through."

Ten minutes later, Charlie and his sworn friend, arm in arm again, marched out of the hotel and wove their way unsteadily up the street toward the swinging doors of the nearest café.

They had a drink in there.

Then they went somewhere else and had another.

And, after that, they went into a third café and had one more.

By that time, only the fact that they were linked arm in arm together prevented them from toppling over.

Charlie's pal waxed merrier the more he drank. The world was colored with the liquor he had imbibed; all was rosy. He announced that he felt a desire to sing stealing over him. The next moment he had launched into a rendition of "It's a Long Way to Tipperary" in a cracked and wavering tenor, as he and Charlie zigzagged along the street.

Charlie himself was in a thoughtful mood. From the sober expression on his face, and his unbroken silence, he seemed to be revolving some deep and weighty matter in his mind—his gravity was as marked as his companion's exuberance of spirits.

Before the entrance of a brilliantly lighted restaurant, Charlie's pal halted, which meant that perforce Charlie halted, too.

"Let's go in here," proposed his companion. "C'mon!"

Charlie allowed himself to be guided, without resistance, into the glittering lobster palace. A waiter escorted them to a table, and hovered about them, with his pencil poised above his pad to take their order.

"Two beers," ordered Charlie's pal.

Charlie nodded gravely.

"And something to eat," he added.

"Sure," echoed his pal. "Something to eat. Fish balls. And liver and bacon. And a whole lemon-meringue pie. Don't forget the beers."

The waiter departed, an awed expression on his face, while his eyes were fixed upon the order he had just been given.

Charlie's companion slapped him between the shoulders.

"Ain't this a great little place, eh?" he asked gayly.

Charlie lifted his hand to his brow unsteadily.

"We're the two sports who are having a high old time to-night—eh, what?" went on the other, slapping him jovially on the back again. "You stick to me, and I'll stick to you, and we'll both stick till the lights go out!"

And he laughed uproariously at his own wit.

At the table beside them sat a Frenchman. Faultlessly attired in a high silk hat, a frock coat, and spats, the noise Charlie's pal was making appeared to displease him, as he sat sipping a glass of wine which was more in keeping with the place than the beer which the waiter had just brought Charlie and his companion.

Charlie lifted his glass, and thoughtfully blew the foam off it onto the carpeted floor. Then, with the same air of thoughtfulness, he took a pull at the glass.

At that moment his pal slapped him between the shoulder blades again.

The beer, which Charlie had not yet swallowed, left his lips in a stream such as might have jutted out of a siphon of vichy—and went squarely into the Frenchman's eye.

The foreigner rose and raised his hat stiffly to Charlie.

Charlie falteringly returned the salute, without arising. Then, picking up the half loaf of bread which the waiter had brought them, he tore off a chunk of the crust and threw it over his shoulder, preparatory to eating the soft part.

The crust of bread struck the Frenchman on his other eye. Again he sprang up. "I will pull your nose, m'sieu," he blurted threateningly to Charlie, "if you insult me again."

At the Frenchman's belligerent tone, Charlie's pal was on his feet in a moment. The next, he was standing before the foreigner, between him and Charlie.

"Don't you hit my pal!" he warned the Frenchman. "Hit me."

The Frenchman drew himself up, and shrugged disdainfully.

"I do not care to make a scene in a public restaurant," said he, "by striking you. But I shall complain to the head waiter, and have you thrown out of here—as you deserve."

He walked stiffly away to carry out his intention.

Now, the head waiter of that fashionable eating place happened to be the husband of the girl with whom Charlie had had all the trouble earlier in the evening. He came back at the Frenchman's heels.

"This is the person," said the latter haughtily, pointing to Charlie's pal.

The burly head waiter walked up to him.

"What's the matter with you?" he asked leniently. "Can't you behave yourself?"

Charlie's defender in the argument which had started between him and the Frenchman bristled militantly before the head waiter, as he had in front of the foreigner.

"Hit me!" he invited the head waiter. "Go on and hit me!"

The head waiter's brows lowered.

"Don't get gay now," he advised, "or I *will* hit you."

"Hit me!" urged Charlie's pal. "Go on—hit me!"

The head waiter obliged him promptly. Charlie's friend went sailing through the air, and landed in a heap at the foot of the staircase beyond the fountain which played in the center of the restaurant.

Scrambling up, he walked unsteadily back to the head waiter.

"Hit me!" he repeated. "Hit me again!"

The head waiter accommodated him a second time. And, a second time, Charlie's pal went back through the air once more, to land at the foot of the staircase.

He picked himself up, and fairly ran back to the head waiter in his eagerness.

"Hit me," he begged, "just once more!"

The head waiter, seizing him by one shoulder, pushed him back against the wall. Then, with his other hand, he slapped him, first on one cheek, and then on the other, four or five times.

Meanwhile, Charlie Chaplin, who was the cause of all the trouble, sat at the table, his little bamboo cane held between his legs, looking thoughtfully before him into space. The head waiter glanced around at him. Charlie, at the same time, looked over his shoulder toward the thickset man who was slapping his pal's face.

Charlie smiled and nodded at him pleasantly, as much as to say, "Hit him as much as you like; don't mind me, old chap."

Releasing Charlie's pal, the head waiter pointed to Charlie, whom he did not recognize, now that he had changed his pajamas for his street clothes, as the man he had chased out of his wife's room earlier in the evening, and said:

"Why don't you try to be nice like your friend? Go back and sit down with him and behave yourself. Or, if you don't, I'll have to put you out of here."

But Charlie's pal, who had revealed himself as a glutton for punishment, wasn't satisfied yet, it seemed.

"Throw me out!" he begged, pushing himself up against the head waiter and looking into the latter's face as appealingly as a dog at his master who holds a bone. "Go on and throw me out!"

The head waiter lost his patience.

"All right," said he, "out you go!"

And, turning him around, he took hold of him by the back of his collar and the seat of his trousers, and ran him up the staircase. At its top landing, pointing him in the direction of the main entrance of the restaurant, the head waiter gave him a push that sent him flying through the air again, to land, this time, on the sidewalk outside the eating place.

Meanwhile, the person for whom the Frenchman had been waiting alone at his table came in and sat down beside him. The person was a girl, and a very pretty one, as Charlie, sitting near by, was not too far gone to recognize.

He smiled at the girl, who paid no attention to him.

Engaged in explaining to the Frenchman the reason for her delay in keeping her appointment with him, she swung the hand bag which she carried with her to and fro in her hand.

There was a little tassel on the end of the bag. And, in its swinging, the tassel tickled the end of Charlie's nose. He blinked, and looked down at the thing as it touched his nose again.

The girl, lowering her arm, so that the bag no longer swung near Charlie's face, continued to swing it back and forth. Charlie, sitting farther down in his chair, slowly opened his knees and watched the bag carefully. As it swung toward him, he snapped his knees shut in an endeavor to catch it.

He missed. He tried again. The same result rewarded his efforts. Then, a third time, he attempted to imprison the bag between his knees, and this time he succeeded.

As the girl tried to swing the bag back, and couldn't, she looked sharply around to see what was holding it, and met Charlie's smile.

"How do you do?" he murmured to her, raising his battered derby by the back of its brim.

She pulled her hand bag out from between his knees, with a haughty lift of her shoulders, and turned back to the Frenchman.

Charlie leaned toward the pair, and began to listen to the story the Frenchman was telling her. He smiled and nodded at each minor point in the recital which the foreign gentleman was making. Finally, when the Frenchman reached the climax of his tale, Charlie, laughing heartily, expressed his approval to the girl by slapping her vigorously between the shoulders.

She bounced around and glared at Charlie, and then appealed to her escort.

The Frenchman, rising, tipped his hat stiffly to Charlie again. And once more Charlie returned the salute without rising.

"This is insufferable!" the Frenchman declared. "The second time I have been annoyed by this—this person! I shall complain at once to the head waiter of him. He shall put him out of here, as he did his companion. One moment, mademoiselle, while I go to see that head waiter. As for you——"

He turned to Charlie, and, drawing off one of his gloves, slapped him across the face with it five or six times in rapid succession.

Charlie coughed behind his hand. He turned to the table beside him. The waiter had brought the food which he and his pal had ordered, and Charlie's eyes fell on the lemon-meringue pie. Picking it up, he poised it on his hand.

And then he threw it at the Frenchman, and the pastry caught the latter squarely in the eyes. The doughy mass of pie covered his face, entirely obscuring the vision of one eye, and plugging his mouth temporarily against speech.

Wheeling, he rushed off blindly to find the head waiter.

Charlie, turning and wabbling off in the opposite direction, reached the fountain. The sight of the water in the basin reminded him that now was as good a time as any for him to perform his ablutions.

Standing at the fountain's brink, Charlie removed his coat and rolled up the sleeves of his shirt. He washed his face, using his handkerchief as a wash cloth, and being careful to do his neck and behind his ears.

Then, wadding the wet handkerchief up in his hands, he threw it over his shoulder behind him.

At that moment the head waiter had returned at the Frenchman's heels, to settle Charlie as he had his pal before him. He was looking around for him, when the handkerchief came flying through the air.

It landed with a wet "plop!" in the middle of his face.

Looking in the direction from which the sopping handkerchief had come, the head waiter saw Charlie at last, and started toward him.

Meanwhile, pulling up one of the leaves of the pond lilies in the basin of the fountain, Charlie examined its root and found it covered with a number of fibrous minor roots. He swished it around in the water, and then brushed his teeth with it.

Bending over as he did so, he was unaware of the fact that the head waiter stood back of him.

The latter, as Charlie straightened up, handed him his derby. Charlie took it without looking around, and clapped it on his head. Then the head waiter handed him his little bamboo cane. Charlie took that with the same indifference—taking the person who was handing him his things to be a coatroom attendant.

The head waiter, picking up his coat, held it out for Charlie to put on. And Charlie did so. Then, feeling in his pocket for a tip, he extracted a nickel and turned to hand it to the person behind him.

He started as he saw the head waiter glowering at him.

The next moment, with a single sweep of his mighty right arm, the latter had knocked Charlie through the air to the foot of the same staircase at which his pal had sprawled three separate and distinct times before.

Picking himself up, Charlie came back toward the head waiter.

As he did so, the latter started to pull off his coat. Charlie took one look at the bulging biceps of the big man, and at his powerful neck and his fine chest expansion. He turned right around on his heels and started up the stairs as fast as he could go—which was at a rate of speed that was astonishingly rapid, considering the fact that only his heels touched the ground.

Walking outside the restaurant, Charlie tripped over his pal, who still lay on the sidewalk, where he had sprawled after leaving the place at the head waiter's urging.

Charlie dragged him to his feet in silence. And then, arm in arm once more, they ambled back to the hotel.

Charlie's pal got the key of their room from the proprietor at the desk, and they mounted to the third floor together, Charlie's friend bending over in the hall to insert the key in their door.

Charlie seated himself on that portion of the other's body which was thrust invitingly toward him as a resting place, and swung his leg while he waited for his friend to unlock the door.

At that moment the wife of the head waiter came down the hall, fully dressed, as she had just returned from attending to an errand that had taken her up the street, and stopped to put her key into the door of her room.

"Ah, there!" Charlie greeted her, with a smile and a tip of his derby.

She turned and favored him with a scornful glance. Then, opening her door, she stepped into the room and slammed the door in Charlie's face.

Charlie got off his friend's back. At that moment the latter had succeeded in unlocking their door, and the release of Charlie's weight from him sent him plunging, headfirst, into the room before him.

Charlie, ignoring him, went to the door through which he had just seen the girl pass. He looked up the hall. Then he looked down it. And then he bent over and looked through the keyhole of that door.

"Oh, my!" breathed Charlie, straightening.

He took off his hat, and fanned his face with it.

Then he bent over again and looked through the keyhole once more. He inserted the tip of his little finger into it, and removed a speck of dust which had got in the way of his vision. After which he applied his eye to the keyhole once more and held it there for two or three minutes.

Standing erect, Charlie coughed, as the banker on the stage always does before going in to the meeting of the board of directors to lay down the law to them—a cough that was designed to rally his fluttering courage to the point of going through with a step he had in mind.

Once more Charlie looked up and down the hall, stepping back from the door as he did so. He pulled down his vest and straightened his necktie and his derby, tucking his cane under his arm.

Then, stepping up to the door, he rapped briskly on it with his knuckles.

There was a pause. And then the door opened.

And out of it stepped the head waiter, who had returned to the hotel from the restaurant by a straighter course—literally and figuratively both—than Charlie and his pal had taken.

"Well?" growled the thickset man, fixing Charlie again with his baleful eye.

Charlie tipped his hat to him, with his mouth hanging open, but no words coming from it. The husband of the girl Charlie had expected to see come to the door of the room placed his hands on his hips.

"Looking for anything?" he inquired of Charlie.

"Oh, no!" said Charlie hastily.

"You're sure of it, are you?" insisted the scowling man.

"Oh, yes; quite sure!" Charlie hurried to set all his doubts at rest on that point. "I—I'm—well, good night!" he finished weakly, and, turning, he marched into the room where his pal was already sound asleep on top of the bed where he had tumbled.

The head waiter followed Charlie into the room, and stood silently at his elbow. Charlie picked up his suit case from the floor and opened it. From the top of the bureau, he tossed his comb and brush and shaving things into the open valise. Then, without looking at the burly, broad-shouldered man who stood frowningly watching him, Charlie pulled open the bureau drawers and dragged out his pajamas, a change of linen, a shirt, collar, necktie, two handkerchiefs, and a pair of socks, and threw them, helter-skelter, into the suit case. After which he closed the grip and locked it. Most of the things were sticking out of the end of it.

Charlie walked to the door of the room and opened it.

The thickset man, in the same frowning silence, followed him to it right at his elbow. Charlie coughed dolefully. Then, with a shrug of his shoulders to the right and to the left, and shifting the position of his feet a few times, Charlie swung his arms out from his sides and let them fall to them again, turned, and walked out into the hall.

Still glued at his elbow, the husband of the girl followed him.

So he and Charlie went downstairs, and so they crossed the lobby to the desk. Charlie did not hesitate there to pay his bill; he left that for his dear old college chum, who was asleep upstairs, to settle when he should awake. The burly man halted there. But Charlie kept right on to the door. On its threshold he paused and looked back over his shoulder.

"Looking for something?" the head waiter inquired eagerly, starting toward him.

Charlie immediately turned.

"Oh, no!" he threw back over his shoulder. "Nothing at all—really!"

And he passed out of the door, and so out of the hotel. On the pavement outside he set down his suit case and walked on for a few steps. Then, remembering that he had left the grip behind him, he retraced those few steps and picked the suit case up again. He wandered on up the sidewalk, with the sleeve of one shirt and the leg of his pajamas trailing out of the suit case behind him.

Charlie Chaplin sighed.

"No more poussé café for mine!" he vowed earnestly. "I'll stick to drinking cocktails made of nitroglycerin, with a stick of dynamite in for a cherry, after this—and avoid trouble."

And Charlie, as he walked on, sighed again.

The Tramp

CHARLIE CHAPLIN came walking down a country road. He was walking rapidly, for him. Which means that he was moving at the rate of approximately one-fifth of a mile an hour. He was walking on his heels, with his toes turned out at right angles, and in using the little bamboo cane that he carried with him to aid his progress, he did not do so in the usual manner, by pushing it against the ground to propel himself on his way, but swung it round and round by the handle, much as though he expected the breeze it stirred up to blow him along, as if he had been a ship.

An automobile horn tooted in Charlie's rear. He kept on walking in the middle of the road, paying no heed to it, for his thoughts were elsewhere. To be exact, they were on a certain dinner he had once eaten.

"The chicken was done to a turn, with the gravy oozing down on the sweet potatoes that were heaped all around it on the platter," mused Charlie, who had not eaten for two days; "and then there was green corn, with June peas and hot biscuits—I remember those biscuits distinctly. And then came apple pie and ice cream and two kinds of coffee, large cups and demitasse, and——"

Charlie jumped sideways into the air and sprawled in the dust of the road, just as the automobile, whose warning blast he had ignored, swept by him.

As he picked himself up, Charlie stepped directly into the path of another motor car that was whizzing along the road from the opposite direction.

By a feat of agility that would have done credit to a professional acrobat, Charlie managed to evade the front wheels of the auto, though by a margin no wider than a hair, and once more he measured his length in the road.

He sighed, as he got to his feet once more and continued his snail-pace walk.

"If I had money," commented Charlie to himself, "I know what I'd do. I'd hire an automobile and a man to run it, and I'd bring it out here. Then I'd walk along in the middle of the road and make it follow me, honking its horn, for ten miles, without getting out of the way once to let it go by."

Charlie Chaplin clapped one hand to the tails of his coat, clutched at his hat with the other, and jumped sideways again. He thought he had heard the tooting of another auto horn back of him. But the sound had existed only in his imagination.

Smiling to himself, Charlie shrugged his shoulders in deprecation of his needless alarm, and swung the bundle he carried in a red bandanna handkerchief in the hand that did not grip his little cane.

In that bundle was Charlie Chaplin's lunch, which a kind woman had handed out to him at the back door of a farmhouse earlier in the day.

Charlie had been carrying the lunch all morning, without being able to decide to break his forty-eight-hour fast with it. As long as he carried it, he would have something to eat. Once he ate it, it would be gone. And there was no telling where his next meal was to come from.

But now Charlie turned into the woods that bordered the road, and seated himself in a glade that was screened from the view of passers-by on three sides by the thick foliage of the bushes and trees. Against the trunk of an oak he leaned back, with the bandanna-wrapped bundle beside him on the grass, and sniffed the air.

There was wafted upon it from somewhere near by the unmistakable aroma of food being cooked.

Charlie Chaplin's little black mustache took a melancholy slant on his upper lip. He drew in his cheeks, which gave an extremely woebegone expression to his face, and lifted his eyes heavenward.

"Beef stew!" he murmured, as one enraptured. "I wish I had some of it, instead of this cold meat and bread, and the two chilled-steel doughnuts I saw that lady put in when she gave me the hand-out!"

Charlie was unaware of the face that was thrust just then through the bushes on his left. A face on which grew a three-weeks-old stubble of reddish-brown beard, and that comprised a nose heavy drinking had colored to the hue of an American Beauty rose, shifting eyes, and a thin-lipped, vicious mouth.

The face belonged to a hobo; but to the type that constables in the small country towns put down on sight as "dangerous," which Charlie, though himself a vagabond, was not.

The tramp who peered out unseen at Charlie from the cover of the bushes was one of a trio of hoboes that were encamped a short distance farther into the woods. It was from their camp fire that Charlie had smelled the beef stew cooking. But if he held the cold lunch beside him in contempt, as compared to a hot meal, the tramp who had come upon him in that glade did not. It would make a welcome addition to the stew his companions were preparing, he felt. And, thrusting his arm cautiously out through the bushes, he laid hold of the bundle.

Drawing it toward him, undetected by Charlie, he quickly untied the bandanna, extracted the cold meat, bread, and doughnuts from it, and then, with a mocking grin, he placed a brick in its stead, tied the bandanna around it as before, and pushed it back to its former place beside Charlie on the grass.

The next moment, the ragged and unshaven rascal was hastening away through the woods, to turn Charlie's lunch into the common commissariat of his equally unscrupulous fellows.

Charlie turned his attention to the bundle. He untied the bandanna, and found the brick. And once more he sighed dispiritedly. This was what he got for not being satisfied with what he had. Now he had nothing at all to eat. Unless——

Pulling up several blades of grass, Charlie Chaplin reflectively chewed them. He took a pinch of salt from his vest pocket and sprinkled it on the next bunch of grass he pulled up. It improved the taste slightly, but not enough to make him relish the fare. Charlie swung the tomato can that was tied to a cord around his shoulders into place before him, dipping his fingers into the water it held and applying them to his lips, as though the can had been a finger bowl.

Then, reflectively examining his hands, Charlie discovered that he was in need of a manicure. Having nothing else to do, as he sat there in the glade, he proceeded to polish his nails.

Just then a girl was walking through the woods, the daughter of a farmer, whose place was situated near by. She was a pretty girl. Approaching the camp of the three hoboes, one of whom had robbed Charlie Chaplin of his lunch, she was unaware of their presence as she looked down at some bills in her hands that her father had given her to turn over to a neighbor in payment for a calf he had bought, and which she was counting as she walked.

The three tramps saw her and the money she held, and they rose to block her path.

"Fork over that dough!" growled one of the three.

With a cry of fright, the girl gave back a step. The three tramps came after her. The red-nosed vagrant, who had despoiled Charlie of his lunch, made a grab at the bills in her hand. The girl evaded his outstretched arm, darted past the other two hoboes, and ran through the woods toward the glade in which Charlie sat, crying for help as the tramps pursued her.

As the girl burst into the glade, Charlie got up from under the tree against which he had been leaning. The farmer's daughter saw that he was a vagabond, like her pursuers. But one glance at Charlie's childlike, innocent face told her that he was one she could trust. She threw herself into his arms.

"Save me!" she pleaded. "Don't let them steal my money!"

The bills in question, which she still held in her hand, tickled the end of Charlie's nose as she wildly embraced him. Charlie, looking down at the greenbacks, tipped his battered derby to them respectfully.

"Don't let who steal your money, Miss Rockefeller?" he asked.

At that moment, the three tramps ran into the glade.

"These rascals," explained the girl. "They tried to snatch it out of my hand, back there in the woods. That's why I ran here—to you. You *will* protect me, won't you?"

Charlie Chaplin turned the girl around in his arms, placing her between him and the three hoboes. He frowned fiercely at them over her shoulder.

"Stand back!" he ordered dramatically. "Who touches a hair of her gray head—— No, that's not the one! I mean, she has sought the protection of Jack Farraday, and who attempts to lay a finger on her will have *me* to deal with!"

The tramp with the rum-blossom nose, who was also the burliest of the three, slowly advanced, with his shoulders lowered in a menacing crouch.

"Cut out d' Third Av'noo melodrammer spiel," he rasped at Charlie, "an' leave go o' dat goil, or yuh'll git hurt! We want dat money she's got. An' we're goin' to git it. See?"

Charlie removed the girl's arms from around his neck, and stepped away from her obediently. But as he did so, he lightly swung the brick in the bandanna handkerchief through the air in an arc, which abruptly terminated on the point of the tramp's unshaven chin.

The hobo's eyes popped wide open and his jaw fell. Gripping the top of his head in both hands, he held on to it as though he feared it was going to sail off like a roof in a cyclone. His knees bending under him, he tottered to the right, then he tottered to the left.

Charlie began to whistle a popular one-step, in accompaniment to the tramp's unsteady progress from side to side of the glade.

And as he whistled, Charlie blithely swung the bundle again. He tapped the nearest of the two other hoboes with the brick in the bandanna. And then he hit the third tramp with it.

The victims of their own evildoing—for if they had not left the brick in the bundle from which they had stolen his lunch, Charlie would have had no weapon to use against them in protecting the girl from their thieving attack—ran off at the top of their heels.

And Charlie ran after them.

He chased the tramps to the edge of a stream. There, seeing him still coming after them with the brick in the bandanna swinging in his hand, they waded out into the water, up to their waists, to escape from the stupefying effects of that improvised missile. Charlie, his head turned with his triumph over them, was about to follow them into the stream, to complete their rout. But he was driven back from the bank by the hoboes, who scooped up mud from the bottom of the stream and threw it at him.

Running backward, to escape from the rain of mud that was aimed at him, Charlie stumbled upon the fire the tramps had left at sight of the farmer's daughter, and sat down in it.

He rose again quickly. The seat of his baggy trousers was on fire. Pulling off his hat, Charlie fanned the site of the conflagration with it. But that only caused the flames to leap higher around his coat tails.

Charlie ran back to the stream, where lay his only hope of putting the fire out.

The hoboes still held the water, however. And again, at sight of Charlie, they flung mud at him with both hands. Charlie turned around and bent over, hoping that a chance shot or two from the enemy would reach the portion of his trousers that was smoldering, and so extinguish the blaze.

But, though his battered derby was knocked off, one of his ears filled with mud, and his collar ruined beyond repair by a chunk of the clay that found a target there, the spot on which he wanted the hoboes to score a hit was left unscathed.

Charlie galloped away, on his heels, in search of some other stream or brook in which he could drown out the fire—looking like a crazy runabout, with the smoke trailing out from under his coat tails as he ran.

At last he found what he was seeking in the mouth of a huge water pipe that protruded from the side of a bank, and out of which ran a thin trickle of water.

Charlie sat down in the mouth of the pipe and remained there until he had cooled off. When he rose and set off through the woods toward the glade in which he had left the girl, his walk was even more of a travesty on a human gait than ever, due to the damage the fire had done to his seating capacity.

"My hero!" the farmer's daughter greeted him. "How can I ever repay you?"

Charlie lifted his arms and brought them down to his sides, in a gesture significant of the fact that he considered what he had done was nothing—a mere trifle.

"You haven't got a ham sandwich with you, have you?" he answered her question, his expression turning anxious. "A chicken wing, or a dill pickle—anything to eat?"

She laughed, and shook her head.

"I guess the point of the joke gets by me," said Charlie gravely. "I don't see anything to laugh at in that. And you wouldn't, either, if it was last Tuesday since you had sat down to a square meal."

Drawing nearer to her, Charlie ran his fingers through the bills which she still held in her hand.

"She loves me, she loves me not," he recited, turning over the greenbacks.

Then, laughing with her, he wriggled his shoulders and tipped his hat again to the money, stepping back. The girl held the bills out to him.

"Let me give this to you," she said impulsively. "You deserve it, and—and you look as though you needed it."

Charlie shook his head in refusal of the offer.

"No," said he, "no. I could take the pennies out of a blind man's cup, or candy away from a baby. But I couldn't take money from you. I don't know why. But I couldn't."

The girl's eyes shone as they rested on him.

"I knew you were honest!" she exclaimed. "And I'll tell you what you do: Come with me and let me introduce you to my father. I'm sure, when he has heard how you have kept those tramps from stealing his money, that he will give you a job."

"A—a job?" faltered Charlie.

"Yes. Aren't you looking for work?"

"Well, not exactly. But if it bumps into me—and leading three meals a day by the hand, too—I suppose I can't avoid it. All right, I'll go with you to your father."

As the girl had said, when her father learned how Charlie had defended his daughter from the hoboes who had tried to rob her of the money with which he had sent her to his neighbor's farm, he was grateful to him for the service he had rendered. And he offered to give him his bed and board, if he would help his hired man with the chores. Charlie hesitated about accepting the offer. But the sight of the kitchen table, laid for dinner, decided him in favor of taking the place.

"But I'm under the doctor's orders," he warned the farmer. "I've got a delicate constitution. And he has told me to look out for any violent exertion. It might cause my heart to stop beating. It would be cheaper for you to be careful of me, and not give me too much work to do, than to have to pay my funeral expenses."

Invited to sit down to the table, Charlie refused.

"I'll eat mine from the mantelpiece," he announced, without explaining that it was because of his unfortunate encounter with the hoboes' camp fire that he preferred not to sit down. "It's a habit I got into when I was in the Peruvian army. So many officers used to come in when we soldiers were eating in the mess tent, and we'd have to get up and salute them each time, that we finally ate standing up. I've never been able to do it any other way since."

And from the mantelpiece Charlie ate his dinner.

Afterward, the farmer handed him a sprinkling pot. Leading him to the door of the farmhouse, he pointed out to Charlie a number of small peach trees that were planted in two rows in the orchard.

"If you don't think the exertion will be too much for you," the farmer ironically told him, "you can water those trees."

Charlie waddled away to them, carrying the sprinkling pot in both hands, and with the strained expression on his countenance that might have been produced there if the can had weighed a hundred pounds.

He started at the first tree of the row nearest the house. Sprinkling that, he walked over to the first tree of the second row. Then he carried the sprinkling pot back to the first row, and from that returned to the second—thus making twice as much work for himself as he had any need of doing.

The farmer, who had been watching Charlie from the doorway of the farmhouse, came out and took the sprinkling pot away from him.

"You'll work yourself to death that way, all right," the farmer told him grimly. "Maybe you'd better go up in the barn and collect the eggs that the hens have laid in the hay—that'll be easier."

Charlie Chaplin, mounting to the hayloft, looked about him in the dusk for eggs. Then he stepped on something in the hay that gave forth a crackling sound, and he knew that he had found what he was seeking. Not alone by the sound of the breaking egg shell did he know it. He had other evidence, as well. Holding his nose, Charlie stooped and gathered up a half dozen of the unbroken eggs into his hat.

A tall young man, with long hair and an open book in his hand, was passing as Charlie emerged from the barn. In impassioned tones, the young man read aloud these lines from the page on which his eyes were preoccupiedly fixed:

Oh, spring! Of all the seasons,
  Summer, winter, fall,
For various personal reasons,
  I love you best of all!
You bring the open trolley cars
  Between the beach and city,
And bock beer into all the bars.
  And so I sing this ditty
To spring, sweet spring——

Charlie Chaplin, as he went by the young man, dropped one of the eggs from his hat into the open book. The young man closed it abruptly, and the egg broke. Immediately he, too, held his nose.

"That's rotten!" he exclaimed.

"I know it is," said Charlie, referring to the "Ode to Spring" the young man had been declaiming. "And that's why I gave you what was coming to you."

Charlie turned the rest of the eggs over to the farmer, who then ordered him to go back with the hired man and get down some sacks of flour from the grain loft in the barn.

Picking up a pitchfork, Charlie walked behind the hired man—whose perpetual expression, by the way, was that of one who has just been waked up out of a sound sleep.

At every other step of the way to the barn, Charlie pricked him with the pitchfork. When they arrived at the foot of the ladder that led up to the window of the grain loft, the hired man, with a prodigious yawn, announced:

"You go up and get down them sacks o' flour. I'm goin' to take a snooze."

"Oh, no!" said Charlie. "*You* go up and get them."

"No, sir," insisted the hired man. "I'm just as lazy as you are."

"But I've got the pitchfork," Charlie reminded him. And he jabbed him with it again. "Go ahead—up you go!"

Forced to obey, the hired man mounted the ladder and disappeared through the grain-loft window. He emerged with a sack of flour on his shoulders, and began the descent. Halfway down the ladder—unaware that the farmer had come to the foot of it to see how they were getting along—the hired man tossed the sack off his shoulders. It hit the farmer, knocking him down, and covering him from head to foot with flour dust.

"Go up and fetch down another sack," the farmer grimly directed the hired man.

As the latter turned and remounted the ladder, the farmer, who had risen from under the sack that had descended upon him, picked up a flat stick from the ground, and waited with it tightly gripped in both hands at the bottom of the ladder.

When the hired man came down within reach, another sack of flour on his shoulders, the farmer swung the stick against that portion of his anatomy which was the most prominently displayed.

The flour sack slipped from his shoulder and fell—on Charlie Chaplin this time, covering him likewise with flour dust.

The farmer announced that enough work had been done for that day. Charlie felt that he would have murdered him if he had asked him to do anything more. After supper—which Charlie again ate standing up—the farmer handed him a candle.

"You can sleep in the attic room with Rufe," he told Charlie, with a nod toward the hired man, who stood beside him.

The flame of the candle which Charlie held was directly under the hired man's chin, but he was too lazy to move his head away from its painful heat.

As soon as they had reached the small room with its one bed on the top floor of the house, Rufe, pausing only to pull off his boots, fell over on the pillows and was instantly fast asleep. He began to snore at the same time. Charlie tried everything, from rolling him over on his side by main strength to covering his open mouth with his hat, in vain attempt to drown out the sound of those thunderous snores which shook the very walls of the room. Giving it up at last, Charlie tried to get to sleep despite the deafening racket. But it was no use. The noise his bedfellow made was enough to banish his own slumber completely.

It was a fortunate thing, however, that Charlie could not get to sleep. For, lying there wide awake, he heard a sound at the window, an hour after the household had all gone to bed. Raising his head, Charlie looked toward the window, and saw the face of the red-nosed hobo, who had stolen his lunch earlier in the day, framed there.

The three tramps, having failed to rob the farmer's daughter, were now bent on robbing his house.

Springing out of bed, Charlie Chaplin ran to the window, threw it open, and pushed the rascally vagrant off the ladder by which he had climbed up to that attic room.

And then, hurrying into his clothes, and shouting to arouse the farmer as he did so, Charlie ran downstairs and out of the house to attempt the capture of the miscreants.

The farmer, having hastily clad himself in trousers and shirt, followed him to the doorway of the farmhouse. Making out a running figure in the dark before him, the farmer clapped the shotgun he had brought with him to his shoulder, and fired.

Part of the load of buckshot was wasted on the night air. But some of it struck Charlie Chaplin in one leg, bringing him down.

He was the one the farmer had aimed at, by accident, and not the hoboes, who had succeeded in making their escape.

But it was through Charlie's efforts that they had not robbed the farmer. And the latter, bringing Charlie into the house, was warm in his praise of his resource and bravery. The farmer's daughter appointed herself Charlie's nurse. And in the days that followed, while he was recovering from his wound, Charlie began to nourish a dream:

It was of one day marrying the pretty girl, and settling down on that farm for the rest of his life.

"Why not?" Charlie asked himself. "She seems to like me. And she's the first girl I've ever met that I believe I've been really and truly in love with. I could make her father give me a half interest in the farm, and then I'd bounce Rufe, one lazy man at a time being enough to have around, and——"

And Charlie went on dreaming. But a week later, being entirely cured of his wound by that time, his dream met with a rude awakening.

Looking out through the kitchen window one evening, he saw the farmer's daughter standing at the gate with a young man. The girl put her arms around the young man's neck and kissed him. Charlie turned away, with a hopeless shrug.

"I guess she only liked me," Charlie said to himself; "that was all. It's my move."

From the mantelpiece, he took down his little bamboo cane and his battered derby. Putting on his hat, he glanced all around the kitchen. Then, tipping his derby to it, he went out of the back door.

Five minutes later, Charlie Chaplin went walking down the country road.

In the Park

CHARLIE CHAPLIN paused on the gravel path in the park through which he was strolling. He paused and sighed. It was a lovesick sigh, for the fresh, green grass and the green leaves and the little birdies singing somewhere out of sight among the latter, all combined to set a strange something stirring in his breast, the something toward which the young man's fancy is wont to turn, so the poet tells us, in the glad, spring season.

Charlie Chaplin twirled his little bamboo cane and looked along the path to the right.

He saw a couple sitting close together on a bench; sitting very close together, indeed. At first glance, the fellow appeared to be a cripple. It seemed that he had only one arm, poor chap! But when Charlie, watching, saw the girl bounce abruptly up against his side, and since she could not have made the movement unaided, it was apparent that the fellow must have thus drawn her to him, in a sudden burst of ardor, with the arm which was out of sight around her waist.

Twirling his cane again, this time more rapidly than before, Charlie coughed dolefully behind his hand and looked the other way.

Here another aggravating sight, in his lovelorn condition, met his eyes. Another couple sat on another bench, in that direction. A nurse girl, with a baby carriage beside her, was the heroine of this love scene. The leading man of the sketch, which might have been entitled "Love, While the Cop's Back Is Turned the Other Way," was an exceedingly fat man, with a straw hat that was two sizes too small for him perched on top of his head, in a way suggestive of a wart on a pickle.

As he looked at this pair the fat man tilted the nurse girl's face toward his with his hand under her chin. Charlie groaned hollowly and closed his eyes.

On the soft, May breeze there was borne to his ears a sound like a spoon being slowly drawn out of a bowl of cold mush.

Charlie turned around, with his eyes still tightly shut, and walked blindly away. He crossed—in disobedience to a "Keep-off-the-grass" sign—the stretch of sward that bordered the park path, at the farther end of which was a fringe of bushes. Before these bushes Charlie halted. And from out of their cover, behind him, crept a tramp.

Charlie felt a hand slipped furtively into his coat pocket, and its fingers groping about against the lining, which, alas, was empty. Keeping his eyes fixed on a point straight before him, Charlie reached out his own hand. He ran it into the coat pocket of the would-be thief who was attempting to enrich himself at his expense. Charlie's fingers encountered a cigarette. He drew it out and put it between his lips. Then he went back for a match, found it, and struck a light. Puffing on the cigarette, Charlie turned to the tramp, who at that moment removed his hand from his pocket, as empty as when it had gone into it.

Charlie smiled pleasantly at the hobo, tipping his hat, and started by him. "Much obliged," said he. "Just my favorite brand. If you pick up another, I'll meet you somewhere, and help you to break the cigarette habit by taking it away from you."

And Charlie ambled on his way. He came back onto the path again, as luck would have it, right beside the bench on which sat the couple whose spooning he had first beheld.

Unobtrusively, Charlie Chaplin sat down on the vacant end of the bench.

"If a man hasn't got the price of a meal," he mentally commented, "he can go some place and smell the cooking. And if I haven't got a girl, I can listen to a fellow who has made love to her. Besides, I might pick up a new method. I'm always willing to learn the best and latest ways of endearing oneself to the fair sex."

The man whose ardent embrace of the girl with him on the bench had at first led Charlie to believe him the one-armed victim of a train wreck, or a premature explosion, or something, looked like a French count.

He wore a black, "spade" beard, and mustaches waxed to needle points, with a frock coat and a silk hat.

Whether he was a member of the nobility or not, there was no question whatsoever as to his nationality. Again bouncing the girl—around whose waist his arm was wrapped—suddenly up against his side, he breathed:

"Ma chérie!"

Rather he growled the endearing term. Charlie started, and paled, not knowing what the words meant, as he heard the tone of concentrated fury in which they were delivered.

Could it be, he asked himself, that what he had intruded upon was not a lovers' tryst, but the opening scenes of a murder which was about to be perpetrated there in that lonely part of the park, before his very eyes?

But Charlie sat down again on the bench, from which he had half risen, as out of the corner of his eye he saw the girl throw her arms around her bearded swain's neck in a perfect abandonment of ecstasy.

"It's just the French method," Charlie smiled reassuringly and leniently to himself. "It frightened me for a minute. I thought he was going to bite her on the wrist and give her hydrophobia. But it's just as I said. This is a splendid opportunity for me to pick up a few pointers on love-making that I may be able to use later on."

And straightway Charlie settled himself to play eavesdropper to the conversation of the couple, who were oblivious to his presence beside them on the bench.

"You are ze sun of my life!" the Frenchman declared.

Charlie giggled, and looked around at the girl. She gave her bearded admirer another hug. When he had got back his breath he continued:

"Ze sun, ze moon, and ze stars!"

The girl rewarded this statement of the immensity of the regard in which he held her by kissing him three or four times in rapid succession. Charlie took off his hat and fanned himself with it.

The Frenchman tried to get on with his flowery avowal of how much she meant in his life, while the girl was engaged in repaying his declaration of boundless affection in osculatory kind.

"How was that?" asked Charlie sharply, having failed to catch his words.

He leaned toward the couple, with his hand behind his ear.

"You are my little cabbage!" the Frenchman stated fervently.

Charlie rocked back and forth on the end of the bench in silent mirth. He pressed his hand to his cheek, and then swept it toward an imaginary bystander in the gesture that accompanies the ejaculation, "Oh, for goodness' sake!" Then he rocked back and forth again, and in so doing he rocked himself off the bench onto the path.

At the sound of his fall the Frenchman sprang up. Scrambling to his feet, Charlie faced him with his disarming smile.

"Pardon me for butting in, Count-ed Out," said he, "but your style of courtship is all wrong. I just heard you address this young and beautiful lady as a cabbage. That may be all right in the country you come from. Maybe cabbages over there are admired, treasured objects; but here, in the city of the flat dweller, cabbages are only used to scent up the dumbwaiter shafts and make the other tenants wish the discovery of its combination with corned beef had never been made. She doesn't look, or—or, that is to say, she's not like a cabbage at all. Now, if you'll let me make the suggestion, I think you ought to compare her to——"

"Canaille!" hissed the Frenchman, drawing himself up to his full, slender height of six feet one. "Begone, or I will scratch your eyes out!"

Charlie, still smiling, shook his head at him reprovingly.

"That wouldn't be according to Marquis of Queensbury rules," he pointed out. "Scratching and biting, and kicking on the shins in the clinches, is barred."

"I snap my fingers at you!" announced the Frenchman disdainfully.

"I knock your hat off!" retorted Charlie.

And, with a swing of his little bamboo cane he suited the action to the words.

The Frenchman picked up his hat and clapped it angrily back on his head.

"*Hein!* You wish to infuriate me?" he demanded excitedly. "You wish to make ze blood of my fighting ancestors boil within me? Voilà! You shall fight me ze duel. I have spoken. Perhaps, m'sieu, you carry weapons about you with which we may settle this little point of honor?"

"No; only this cane," replied Charlie.

And with it he knocked the Frenchman's hat off again.

Helpless anger gained complete sway over the tall foreigner. He burst into tears, and jumped up and down on the path like a fractious child.

"I tear my hair!" he announced, in a voice which rage had pitched to a shrill, falsetto key. "You intrude upon my tête-à-tête with mademoiselle! You knock off my hat! You do it again! You have driven me mad! Remorse for having sent me to a lunatic asylum for the rest of my life, m'sieu, shall be your punishment!"

Charlie turned to walk away.

"I won't grieve myself to death over that," he lightly informed the other. "A comical college is where you belong, all right; but I had nothing to do with driving you crazy. You were balmy on the filbert when I met you. Ta-ta, old dear!"

And Charlie strolled along the path toward the nurse girl and her fat admirer, on the bench in the other direction.

On the way Charlie encountered a frankfurter vender, who stood on the path with his can of "hot dogs" resting on the ground beside him, counting up his day's receipts.

Charlie halted at his elbow. He sniffed the air, which was scented with the pungent aroma of the frankfurters in the nickel-plated steamer, and a doleful expression settled down on Charlie's face. He shrugged his shoulders, running his finger around between his neck and his collar.

"Food!" he breathed weakly. "How long has it been since I last tasted you?"

While he stood there, unperceived by the hot-dog merchant—who was engrossed in counting up the loose silver in his hand—and, to all appearances, interested solely in an inspection of the surrounding scenery, Charlie reached down the crooked end of his cane and hooked it around the handle of the steamer's cover.

He lifted the cane, and the cover rose with it.

Inserting his hand into the steaming can, Charlie withdrew it. He held a link of frankfurters, numbering six or seven. Silently replacing the cover on the steamer, Charlie turned and walked away. He had tucked one of the frankfurters in the outside breast pocket of his coat; the rest hung down on his front like the loose end of a watch chain.

Around a bend in the path, out of sight of the vender from whom he had taken the sausages, without the formality of paying for them, Charlie halted, and took a bite of the nethermost frankfurter on the chain.

Then he stood there and began to play a game with himself. He swayed from side to side, thus causing the string of frankfurters that depended from his breast pocket to swing back and forth like the pendulum of a clock. The game was to take a bite of the frankfurter on the end of the swaying link as it swung up to his mouth, without using his hands to assist him in any way.

The frankfurters hit him on the nose, knocking his hat askew on his head. Righting his derby, Charlie snapped at the swinging frankfurters again; and again he missed. The sausages rapped him once more, on the other side of his nose. Shrugging, Charlie gave up the game, as one that was too hard for him to master without more practice, and, the frankfurters still dangling from his pocket, he turned and walked back along the path in the direction for which he had been heading before his meeting with the vender—toward the nurse girl who sat on the bench with the fat man in the little straw hat.

He was not sitting there beside her any longer, Charlie saw as soon as he rounded the bend in the path and came in sight of the bench once more.

The nurse girl occupied it alone. Glancing around, Charlie spied the fat man standing at another bend in the path ahead, beside the frankfurter vender, from whom he was in the act of purchasing one of the frankfurters.

Charlie's eyes traveled back to the nurse girl. She was reading a book. Its title was "Why They Married." Again Charlie's glance traveled speculatively toward the fat man, who was just beginning on his third frankfurter. With another shrug, Charlie approached the girl, who was absorbed in her book.

"She's romantic," he informed himself, "and it will be a treat to her to look up suddenly and find me—the ideal of her dreams—sitting beside her on that bench. I suppose she's only been letting that clumsy specimen of pork on the hoof hang around her because she couldn't find anybody better to spoon with. But he'll be thrown into the discard once she sees me."

Cautiously, Charlie seated himself on the end of the bench beside her.

The nurse girl went on reading, unaware of his presence. Charlie glanced at the open page of the book. His eyes caught a line, traveled on to the next, and in another moment he, too, was absorbed in the recountal of the hero and heroine's relentless pursuit by the villain.

The girl turned over a page. Charlie reached out and turned it back again.

"Wait! I haven't finished that yet!" said he.

She closed the book and jumped up.

"How dare you?" she indignantly demanded.

Charlie, flashing her his most alluring smile, tipped his hat.

"It's lovely May we're having for weather, isn't it?" he blundered, in an attempt to open the conversation gracefully. Then, laughing quickly at his own mistake, he started to correct it. "I mean—that is to say—oh, you know what I mean! But what's a sentence without sense between friends, eh?"

The nurse girl sat down, with a disdainful bounce, on the bench again. She turned her back on Charlie and reopened her book.

"You'd better walk back to the menagerie," she said, with bludgeonlike sarcasm, "where you escaped from."

Charlie sat down beside her once more.

"I'll try the French method," he said to himself. "Maybe it will melt her. It won't do any harm to try it out on her and see how it works." Seizing the nurse girl around the waist, Charlie drew her fiercely to him, growling in her ear: "My sherry!"

The next minute, his head ringing from a box on its side, Charlie found himself sprawling on the path. The girl stood over him, beside the bench from which she had risen.

"I *thought* you were intoxicated!" she announced angily. "You've had so much to drink, you think you're still lined up before a bar, and that I'm a glass on it. I'm *not* your sherry, or your cocktail, high ball, or beer, either, whichever it was that you got this jag with. But if you don't get away from here, I'll call for my young man, and then *you'll* think *you're* a whisky smash. He'll knock your head off!"

Charlie, picking himself up, faced her with unshaken good nature.

"Come, now," he urged, "you must confess that you like me better than him? Why, he's too fat!"

"Not to punch you into the middle of next week!" retorted the nurse girl. She favored Charlie with a withering glance from head to foot, and then seated herself on the bench again. "Splinter!"

Charlie sat down beside her once more.

"All right," he accepted her disdainful appellation. "But, like a splinter, I'm going to stick around."

He draped one leg caressingly across her lap.

"Let's get chummy," he suggested, "and tell each other our first names. Mine is——"

"Your name'll be mud in another minute," she informed him, rising once more. She turned to call to the fat man, whose place beside her on that bench Charlie had attempted to take, and found him standing behind her. He was chewing on the last of the frankfurters he had just returned from buying—for himself, without bringing any for her.

His selfishness, however, did not seem to have cost him anything in her eyes.

"Make him go away!" she ordered, pointing to Charlie. "He's been annoying me all the time you were gone."

The fat man planted himself in front of Charlie. He began to expand his chest. It emerged from his coat, then the vest under it, and continued to swell out until it seemed that it must burst the buttons on his shirt. Charlie raised his arms and let them fall against his sides in a hopeless gesture.

"You're a better man than I am, Gordon Gin!" he misquoted, turning away. "I'll go away somewhere and drown myself. Will that do?"

The fat man frowned at him in silence.

"Good morning, then!" And Charlie, taking his glower to mean assent to his humble inquiry, faced about and walked off.

In the meantime, the tramp whose pocket Charlie had picked of the cigarette and the match, while he was exploring Charlie's own coat in a vain attempt to find something worth taking in it, had come upon the Frenchman and the girl, who were spooning on the bench.

The girl's pocketbook was lying on the seat beside them. Perceiving that the couple, locked in each other's embrace, were oblivious to all that went on around them, the tramp, as he passed by, deftly "lifted" the purse from the bench and dropped it into his pocket.

A moment later he and Charlie met once more on the path.

The tramp saw the frankfurters dangling from Charlie's breast pocket. Being hungry, he attempted to steal them. While he was doing so, Charlie spied the pocketbook, whose handle was sticking out of the hobo's pocket. He took hold of it by the crook of his cane, and when he and the tramp parted company Charlie had again come off the better of the two from their encounter.

The girl, reluctantly withdrawing from the Frenchman's embrace, informed him that it was time for her to go home. She looked for her pocketbook, and discovered that it was gone. The Frenchman rose with alacrity to start in search of the thief.

At that moment the tramp became aware that the pocketbook was gone from his pocket, and that Charlie must have taken it.

He saw Charlie moving away, with the purse dangling from the end of his cane. The hobo started in pursuit of him, loosing a yell of baffled rage as he did so.

Charlie, attracted by the shout, stopped and looked behind him. He saw the tramp running toward him. Stooping, Charlie picked up a brick and threw it at the vagrant. His aim was excellent. The tramp suddenly lost all interest in Charlie, the pocketbook—all other things, as a matter of fact.

He fell over backward on the sward and lay still.

Charlie threw another brick at him for good measure. The Frenchman got in the way of it. With a moan, he sank back on the bench from which he had just risen, his chin falling on his breast, and his eyes closing, as unconsciousness descended like a curtain between the world and his slumbering senses.

Charlie turned and walked on, with the pocketbook hanging from the handle of his cane, behind him.

He passed the fat man, who, perhaps, had gone looking for the frankfurter vender again.

Seeing the purse swinging at the end of Charlie's cane, the fat man took it off as Charlie went by. Feeling the lightening of the end of the cane, Charlie stopped, and smilingly requested him, by signs, to hang the pocketbook back on it again.

The fat man complied, and raised his hat apologetically.

Charlie returned the salute by the back of the brim of his battered derby.

Then he was about to move on, but the fat man caught him detainingly by the sleeve.

"Where did you get it?" he asked, with a nod at the pocketbook.

"Oh, I found it." Charlie told him what was half the truth, at least.

"Have you opened it yet?"

"Not yet."

"You don't know what's in it, then?"

"Correct."

The fat man reached out his hand for the purse.

"Let me look in it," he requested, "and I may buy it from you."

"No, no!" Charlie smilingly shook his head. "If you want to buy it, you'll have to do so in the dark, as they say. You may get stuck—but so may I, for selling it to you too cheap."

While this conversation was going on Charlie and the fat man were both unaware of the fact that a policeman stood not a foot in back of them, listening to all they said.

"How much do you want for it?" the fat man asked.

"Two dollars," Charlie answered.

"That's too much," protested the other. "Keep the pocketbook."

He did not know, and neither did Charlie, that the tramp, who had recovered from the stunning effects of the collision of the brick which Charlie had thrown at his head, had ranged himself up on the other side of them.

"Give me a dollar, then," said Charlie, "and it's yours."

The fat man handed him the sum. Charlie gave him the pocketbook; and then the cop pulled Charlie's sleeve. Putting out his hand blindly, Charlie felt the brass buttons and the shield of the officer of the law behind him. Without a word, he handed the fat man back his dollar. The latter, looking around at the policeman, returned the pocketbook to Charlie in the same silence; and Charlie, catching sight of the tramp for the first time, handed the purse on to him and started to walk away.

The policeman caught him by the slack of the trousers and pulled him back.

"What are you three doing with a lady's pocket-book?" the cop demanded of the other two.

Charlie seized the opportunity to walk around the three and off up the path. As he did so, with the crook of his cane he again withdrew the purse from the pocket of the tramp, where the latter had stuffed it, and walked away with it.

The nurse girl rose, with flashing eyes, from the bench as Charlie approached it.

"You're back again, are you?" she began exasperatedly.

But the angry tone faded out of her voice as she caught sight of the pocketbook which Charlie took off the end of his cane at that moment. Smiling at him, she came close to his side.

"Where did you get that?" she asked.

Charlie shrugged his left shoulder and then his right. He looked all around him, and then, slipping his arm around the nurse girl's waist, he sat down on the bench with her, unreproved this time for his boldness.

"It's a pretty thing, isn't it?" he inquired, holding the pocketbook up for inspection by its handle.

"Where did you get it?" the girl repeated.

"I found it," Charlie answered. "Then I sold it. Then I bought it back again. Then I gave it away. And then I found it again." He laughed lightly, turning to glance at the girl's bewildered face. "It sounds like a riddle, doesn't it? But here's another funny thing about it: I don't know what's in it—maybe nothing, and maybe as much as a dollar and thirty cents."

Swinging the purse around by the handle, he hung his leg over the nurse-girl's lap again, and this time she did not reprove him for that, either.

"In that case," Charlie resumed, "I'd have a dollar and thirty-five. Would you come to a picture show with me this afternoon, then, little girl? Of course you'll understand that I didn't invite you if there's nothing in it but a powder puff, a looking-glass, two spools of thread, some samples of dress goods, and a recipe for getting rid of blackheads, clipped out of the woman's page of the newspaper——"

"It's a pretty pocketbook," interrupted the nurse girl, regarding it with wistful admiration, "whether there's any money in it or not."

Looking up, Charlie saw the cop and the fat man and the tramp coming that way. He removed his leg from the girl's lap, and rose, handing her the pocketbook as he did so.

"Do you like it?" he said abstractedly. "You can have it."

And he walked away in the direction of the lake.

There, on the brink of the placid expanse of water, he found the tall, thin Frenchman, with his beard and waxed mustaches and high silk hat.

He, like the tramp, had shaken off the soporific effects of the brick which Charlie had thrown at the hobo, but that he had received on the temple, instead.

The Frenchman, pacing up and down at the lake's edge, was wringing his hands distractedly. Charlie, halting, saw him remove his hat and place it on the grass. Then he took off his frock coat and folded it and laid it beside the hat on the sward.

"My goddess loses her pocketbook!" Charlie heard him groan aloud to the surrounding trees. "I seek to recover it for her—as I, her knight, should do. Conceive the result! I, Armand Henri Louis Baptiste de Brie, son of France, fail—fail because a brick is thrown and my head gets in ze way! Ah, *misérable!* But I have lost all in her eyes. She despises me now. There is but one thing left for me to do: I must end my life, here and now!"

Charlie, who had drawn nearer, clasped his cheek.

"In this lake I will plunge, and drown my sorrow!" the Frenchman declaimed to the trunk of a near-by oak. "Yes, I will jump in—but, alas, I am afraid!" he faltered, drawing back from the brink over which he had bent to carry out his suicidal threat.

Looking around, he caught sight of Charlie's horror-stricken face.

"Ah, my friend!" cried the Frenchman, running up to him. "I appeal to you! Help me to die!"

At once Charlie's manner became wholly businesslike. Escorting the Frenchman back to the brink of the lake, he instructed him to bend over. Then he drew back and surveyed the other's stooping form measuringly. He moved the Frenchman a foot or so to the right, stepping back once more to view him. Then he nodded as though satisfied.

"Are you all set?" he inquired.

The Frenchman's only response was a quivering moan.

"Any parting messages you want delivered?" Charlie asked solicitously.

The Frenchman, shaking his head, groaned again.

"Then here you go!" said Charlie, and he delivered a kick on that portion of the Frenchman's anatomy which was most prominently displayed, a kick that sent him sailing far out over the lake, to drop into the deep water beyond the bank.

Charlie pulled down his trousers leg, which the force of the kick had disarranged, and straightened with an air of conscious virtue displayed in a good deed carried out.

"It's doing a little act of kindness for a fellow man," he informed himself, "that makes one feel happy and contented with life."

Then Charlie turned around, to find the cop and the fat man confronting him.

"You come along to the station house," the policeman ordered him sternly.

"I've a good mind to punch your nose," chimed in the fat man, stepping menacingly toward Charlie. "Passing stolen goods on to my girl, and trying to get her into trouble——"

Charlie stepped aside, placing the fat man between himself and the brink of the lake. He appealed to the policeman:

"Don't let him hit me, officer!"

The policeman stepped between Charlie and the fat man, and thus he, too, was on the lake side of Charlie; and with a well-directed shove of his hand, Charlie sent, first the fat man, and then the policeman after him, sprawling into the water.

Then, swinging his little bamboo cane, Charlie walked away.

"I wonder if she's opened the pocketbook yet?" Charlie murmured to himself as he strolled back toward the bench on which he had left the nurse girl. "And whether that date for the picture show this afternoon is on or not? I *hope* there was money in the thing!"

A Jitney Elopement

CHARLIE CHAPLIN was waiting for something to turn up—as usual. While he waited, he took a cigarette paper out of one glove and a five-cent bag of tobacco from the other, and proceeded to roll a cigarette. He did it with his gloves on. His eyebrows worked up and down, and his ridiculous little mustache shifted from side to side. He threw some of the scattered tobacco over his left shoulder—to keep off bad luck.

A young and beautiful girl came out on the balcony of the house behind him. She stamped her foot, with a toss of her head, as though in emphasis of a refusal she had just given to obey the order of some one inside that grand mansion. Then, coming to the balcony's rail, she looked down, and, by chance, her glance rested on Charlie Chaplin standing beside the garden wall.

She clasped her hands.

"How brave he looks!" breathed the girl; "how noble and true! His clothes are shabby, I must admit, but that only shows how different he is from the men of society I have known!"

Meanwhile, Charlie Chaplin had raised one leg to bring into view a long-unshined shoe, while he struck a match along a fold of his baggy trousers, to light the cigarette which he had painstakingly made. Most of the tobacco had rolled out of it during the process of its manufacture, and the paper burned in a twinkling down to within a quarter of an inch of his mustache.

A look of hopelessness came into his eyes. He twirled his little bamboo cane to try to regain his composure, but the effort was in vain. With the corners of his mouth drooping despondently, he puffed on the stub of the cigarette which remained between his lips. It was no longer lighted. The rest of the tobacco flew out in the disconsolate sigh he gave, and the empty paper which adhered to his lips flapped up and down against them as he tried to dislodge it by moving his mouth to and fro.

"He shall save me!" whispered the girl, wheeling to run back into her room. There she snatched up paper and pencil, and wrote a note.

Then, returning to the balcony, she found Charlie still standing where she had first seen him. "My hero!" she murmured fondly.

And, crumpling the missive into a ball, she threw it down to him.

It struck him on the mouth, knocking off the cigarette paper. He started, and drew himself up, blinking his eyes rapidly.

Turning, he looked up at the girl. She was pretty, he saw. At once a pleased smile broke over his face. He lifted his hat to her by the back of the brim. Then he looked down at the note on the ground near his feet. He pulled it closer with the handle of his cane, and bent and picked it up.

These were the lines he read:

"My father has written a letter to Count de Ha Ha whom he has never seen, offering him a million dollars and my hand in marriage. I do not love the count. Can't you think of a way to help me?"

Charlie Chaplin wriggled his shoulders. He looked up again at the girl on the balcony. She was a peach; there was no mistake about that! And a million dollars—he whistled an aimless tune, and twirled his bamboo cane at a furious rate.

"Do I need a million dollars?" he asked himself. "Yes! Can I get it by passing myself off as this count? Maybe. Shall I try it? I will!"

He took two little steps forward, stopped to tip his hat again to the girl, and then briskly walked away on his heels.

He rang the front-door bell of the mansion.

"Tell the boss," he informed the tall, sleepy-looking footman who answered the summons, "that Count de Ha Ha has arrived for the million and his daughter."

Two minutes later, he was escorted into the presence of the father of the beautiful heiress.

The gentleman rose and put on his eyeglasses. He looked the visitor over in surprise, taking in his battered derby hat, the shiny black coat and trousers of antique style, and the frayed necktie "riding" the collar.

"You are Count de Ha Ha?"

"Yes, yes!" The trampish intruder tipped his hat rapidly up and down to the millionaire. "Count de Ha Ha—ha, ha!—how d'ye do, how d'ye do!"

The uncertain expression on the other's face lifted.

"A little eccentric," he told himself, as he advanced welcomingly; "but that is to be expected of a foreigner." He warmly grasped both the caller's hands in his. "Delighted to make your acquaintance, count!

You got my letter, I presume? In it I stated that I would give you a million dollars to marry my daughter. Is the arrangement satisfactory to you? But don't—don't decide hastily to reject the offer, my dear count! Wait until you have seen what my daughter looks like. I will go and inform her that you are here. And about that million——"

With a reassuring wave of his hand, Charlie Chaplin seated himself beside a table on which stood a half-filled decanter.

"Get it ready," he directed cheerfully. "I'd accept it if your daughter was the twin sister of Stupid Stephen, here"—jabbing the end of his cane against the vest of the footman, who, with the solemn-faced butler, stood beside his chair. "And," he called after the owner of the mansion, "I'd like to have it all in one-dollar bills, if you don't mind."

The latter laughingly shook his head at him from the threshold.

"Ah, you will have your little joke, count!"

"I may have my little million, too," commented the pretended nobleman under his breath, "if I can keep on getting away with it like this."

Then, looking at the amber-colored contents of the cut-glass decanter at his elbow, he exclaimed aloud:

"Why, dear me—this can't be something to drink?"

"Would you care for a little, sir?" inquired the footman.

Charlie Chaplin smiled his winning smile, as he watched the servant begin to pour out a drink from the decanter into a tumbler.

"Oh, only a little!" he protested. But he gave the decanter a push with the end of his cane, which caused the glass to run half full. "Never mind about pouring it back now. That would spoil it. There's only one thing to do, and that's for me to pour it *down*."

And he suited the action to the words.

"A cigar, sir?" invited the butler.

He was proffering a box at his opposite side. Charlie took a handful and stored them in his hat for future use.

And then he rose to follow the footman, who had left the room, to return with the announcement that the master of the house, with his daughter, was awaiting the visitor's presence in the next room.

Charlie Chaplin found the millionaire rubbing his hands with expectant satisfaction as he stood beside the girl of the balcony. She quickly nodded her smiling understanding of, and willingness to share in, the deception the young man was practicing for her sake.

"Count de Ha Ha," said her father, "allow me to present my daughter Elma."

Chaplin, with the handle of his cane hooked absent-mindedly around the neck of the footman, acknowledged the introduction:

"Suffocated with pleasure!"

He took off his hat, and the cigars fell out.

"A little idea of my own!" he hastily informed the millionaire, biting his lip over the accident. "I always carry my cigars in my hat—yes, yes! I comb my hair with water. It makes my head a first-rate humidor, you see!"

The owner of the mansion crossed to his side, still rubbing his hands.

"Isn't she beautiful, count?" he whispered. "Are you satisfied to marry her now at my terms?"

Chaplin regarded the girl approvingly.

"I'd do it for half a million," he told her father.

The butler appeared in the doorway.

"Dinner is served, sir," he announced.

The millionaire drew his arm through the supposed Count de Ha Ha's.

"You'll stay for dinner, count, won't you?" he urged.

"Oh, yes, yes!" quickly assented Chaplin—it was more than two days since he had had anything to eat. "I always stay to dinner. Even when I come before breakfast, in the morning, I always stay to dinner. I love dinner! Which way is the dining room?"

His host led the way to it with Elma.

Chaplin plucked a flower from the floral centerpiece on the table, salted it, and ate it. He noticed the millionaire was frowningly watching him. Realizing that he had invited detection in his masquerade by the faux pas, in his confusion he sugared his soup, which the butler had just set in front of him. Then, seeing what he had done, to cover the mistake before his host could notice it, he started to dash pepper into it.

He shook the shaker so hard that both Elma and her father began to sneeze. Chaplin's mortification deepened. If he made any more of these blunders, he was *not* going to get away with it, that was certain. He picked up his spoon, to commence eating the soup—and the butler removed the plate before he could do so.

Thus far, he had taken the edge off his hunger with just one simple little daisy of the fields, eaten with salt.

"Will you cut the bread, count?" asked the millionaire.

Charlie Chaplin grabbed up the whole loaf and a knife.

"The bread—certainly, certainly!"

He proceeded to slice the knife into it, without looking at what he was doing.

"How many meals," he asked his host, trying to distract the latter's thoughts from his breaches of table etiquette, by aiming a running fire of conversation at him, "how many meals are there in a million dollars, do you know? I was always good at geography at school. But long division was my weakness. The teachers said——"

He looked down at the loaf of bread in his hands, to find that he had run the knife in a spiral course through its entire length, without severing a single slice from it.

He opened the thing out, and closed it again, like a concertina.

"She was 'bread' in old Kentucky!" he sang gayly, though his heart was quaking for fear he had given himself away for good this time. "Have a hunk?" He tore off half the loaf, and tossed it across the table to the girl's father. "It's the way we always serve bread in Bulgaria," he explained, "where my estate is."

"Bulgaria?" exclaimed the millionaire, putting down his knife and fork beside the steak which the butler was handing around. "I understood you came from France, count!"

"On my father's side," the caller corrected, with another miserable attempt at light-heartedness, though a cold perspiration was beginning to break out on his brow. "I am a vulgarian—I mean a Bulgarian."

He attacked his steak, to find that it was tough as shoe leather.

"Some of the beans, count?" inquired his host.

"Some of the what?"

"Beans."

"Oh, yes, yes!" By mistake, he passed his piece of steak instead of the plate. "I'll have a couple of beans!"

Meanwhile, with a discordant "blat" of the horn, a jitney auto had stopped in front of the entrance to the mansion. Its solitary occupant, the *real* Count de Ha Ha, sprang out and ran up the steps with such haste that he fell all the way down them again. Picking himself up, he finally arrived at the front door, and rang the bell.

"Announce ze Count de Ha Ha!" he breathlessly informed the sleepy-looking footman. "Queek! I have just received your master's letter—I accept! I accept! I will take his daughter off his hands for ze million!"

The footman entered the dining room, to convey to the owner of the house the whispered information of the distinguished caller's arrival.

Charlie Chaplin did not notice the interruption. He had just taken a gulp of the tea which the butler had set down in front of him. It was so hot that the steam came out of his nose. He clapped his napkin over his mouth with one hand, while with the other he cooled down the remainder of the beverage in the cup by dropping a dozen lumps of sugar into it.

The millionaire, following the footman from the room, received the real Count de Ha Ha in the library.

"You are the Count de Ha Ha?" he inquired; but the puzzled look lifted from his face as he saw the caller's silk hat, frock coat, and the monocle in his eye. "Yes, I see what has happened," he quickly went on, his brows coming together in an angry frown. "I have been led to receive a bogus count—allowed myself to be tricked, bamboozled, by a shabby, down-at-heel sharper. But he shall answer to me for it. Wait here for a moment, count."

He returned to the dining room, and brought back Charlie Chaplin into the library.

"Little million dollars," said the latter softly under his breath, when he caught sight of the genuine count, "good night! Also, lovely Elma, there will be no wedding bells for thee and me!"

He stepped up to the millionaire and tipped his hat to him. Then he turned around and obligingly bent over.

"I'm afraid I must leave you," said he. "Kick me good-by!"

With a vengeance, the father of the heiress did so. Charlie Chaplin straightened up, his hat slipping over one eye.

He coughed into his hand, straightening his derby and his tie. Then he twirled his little bamboo cane. And, without warning, he let his foot fly out behind him, to catch the millionaire between the fourth and fifth buttons of his vest, sending him back through the portières as though he had been shot out of a cannon, to fall in a heap into a chair in the next room.

Charlie Chaplin approached the count. He stopped in front of him, and his little black mustache moved from side to side. Then he whacked off the nobleman's high hat with his cane, and passed out of the house.

The millionaire came running back into the room.

"Has he gone?" he demanded. "Well, we don't need to worry about him any more. But, thank heavens, you arrived in time, count! I will go and bring my daughter in for you to see. I am sure you will like her, count."

But Elma did not like *him.* She emphatically said so.

"I don't care whether the other one was a real count or not," she told her father. "I love him, and he is the only man I will ever willingly marry—so there!"

The Count de Ha Ha drew the millionaire aside.

"I have my auto outside," he suggested eagerly. "Let us all three take a leetle spin out into ze country —yes, no? Ze beautiful young lady may be placed in a more yielding, tender mood by ze charm of ze nature."

The owner of the mansion went to get his coat and hat, and ordered the girl to do likewise.

"A good idea, count!" he approved. "You will win her there, while the birdies in the treetops chirp an accompaniment to the persuasion of your gifted tongue, I am sure!"

A half hour later, the party left the jitney auto at a country roadside.

Charlie Chaplin had wandered out to that particular spot himself, after leaving the house. He had missed the million; but that did not make him half so sad as the thought of giving up the girl.

And then he caught sight of her, coming along between her father and Count de Ha Ha, who was heading for a bench that stood under a tree—which he probably thought would be a good place to make his proposal.

"I *won't* give her up!" Charlie Chaplin declared in an undertone. "Not until I have had another try for her, at least."

The Count de Ha Ha had dusted off the bench with his handkerchief, and gracefully bowed an invitation to the girl to seat herself there.

Her father, rubbing his hands again, stole off on tiptoe, to perch himself on a stone wall out of earshot.

Charlie Chaplin started to walk away in the opposite direction, looking for a brick.

Two "dopey"-looking policemen appeared from the neighboring bushes. They lined up on either side of him. Charlie Chaplin walked forward, for three steps, between them. Then he began to walk backward. The two ivory-headed cops continued to saunter along, unconscious of the fact that the "suspicious character" they were accompanying was no longer between them.

The Count de Ha Ha, seating himself beside the girl, leaned toward her fervently and took her hand.

"Ah, mademoiselle!" he began his impassioned plea for her heart.

A brick bounced from his head—for Charlie Chaplin had found what he was looking for.

With a low moan, the count fell over the back of the bench, and lay senseless.

"My hero!" cried Elma, rising, with shining eyes and clasped hands. "Oh, you are going to save me yet!"

She had caught sight of Charlie, quickly walking toward her across the field on his heels. He stood before her, with a smile, and tipped his hat up and down on his curly head.

At that moment the count came to.

"Ha!" he hissed, picking himself up and coming between Charlie and the girl, "You chuck ze brick—yes? Weeth it you lay zis egg here?" he pointed to the lump, the size of an English walnut, which stood out on his brow. "Then I fight you ze duel!"

"No, no!" cried Elma in alarm.

"Why, I thought I put you down for the count, count?" said Charlie Chaplin pleasantly. "About that duel: I'll fight you at ten o'clock in the morning the second Monday of next week—ta-ta!"

As he spoke, he kicked out behind him.

The count went sailing through the air, to collide with the millionaire, who sat reading his newspaper on the stone wall fifty yards away. They both went down in a heap.

A burly, lantern-jawed policeman stood at Charlie Chaplin's side. Charlie caught the girl's hand in his.

"Come on, let's run!" he said, and pulled her after him.

The count, picking himself up once more, helped his prospective father-in-law to his feet.

"Queek!" he cried to the latter. "He has turned up again—that rascal. And now, look! He ees running off with your daughter. We must stop them!"

They bolted after the fleeing couple. As they dashed past the thickset cop, they shouted to him to join them, and he did so. With two hundred yards head start, Elma and Charlie were running, hand in hand, toward the roadway.

"The count's auto!" exclaimed the girl. "We can get away in that!"

She scrambled into the waiting machine. Chaplin, halting his wild run on one leg, started to follow her, tripped over the step, and fell on the road. He got up and clambered aboard the auto. He tugged at this lever and that. But the thing wouldn't start. And behind them they could hear the shouts of their pursuers coming nearer every minute.

"Oh, I know!" Elma cried. "It's a jitney auto. You have to start it with a nickel—have you got one?"

"Yes," said Charlie Chaplin—"one."

He fished the coin out of his pocket.

"It's a buffalo nickel," he told her, as he dropped it in the slot, "just what we need, if they're going to be buffaloed by seeing us ride away from them in this."

The auto started away with a jolt. Charlie Chaplin looked over his shoulder to wave a derisive farewell to the count, the cop, and the father of the heiress at his side, as the three ran out on the road behind them.

"There's another auto up the road," the policeman pointed out. "If we can get the use of it, we may be able to catch them yet."

The trio raced to the waiting car. They pulled out of the rear seat the man who was sleeping there, and dumped him out on the road. Then they piled in and started after the jitney runabout.

Looking behind him, Chaplin saw them coming. He hitched himself back and forth on the seat, to try to make the machine go faster. But, as they swung off the country road onto the smooth boulevard that led back to the city, whose buildings were now plainly in view, the bigger auto was steadily gaining on them.

Charlie Chaplin stopped the runabout. He hopped out, and gathered an armful of bricks. Then he sprang aboard the car again and rode on with the girl.

As he heard the snorting of the auto behind them, he picked up a brick and kissed it for luck, tossing it back over his shoulder.

It struck the policeman, and knocked him out in the back seat.

Chaplin tossed another brick into the air behind him.

It got the count this time, who toppled over on top of the cop.

Around a corner Charlie Chaplin steered the runabout. The bigger touring car followed. He stopped and waited for the other auto to come up. Then he backed into it. The touring car, with Elma's father at the wheel, shot back along the road for a couple of hundred yards from the impact.

"One good shove deserves another," Charlie Chaplin told the girl. "And straight ahead is the place for the next."

He nodded toward a dock at the edge of the river, and ran his machine for it. Back came the other auto in pursuit. Charlie Chaplin waited until it was between him and the river. And then he reversed the lever in his hand again.

The touring car went over the end of the dock, and disappeared in the water.

"Father will never forgive you now!" said the girl, giggling.

"Yes, I've just thrown a million dollars overboard," the young man ruefully agreed. Then his face cleared.

"But I'd call it square," he declared, "for a nickel. Have you got one?"

"Yes," nodded Elma, looking perplexed. "But what do you want with it?"

"To drive you to a parson," said Charlie Chaplin.

THE END.

A CATALOG OF SELECTED

DOVER BOOKS

IN ALL FIELDS OF INTEREST

A CATALOG OF SELECTED DOVER BOOKS IN ALL FIELDS OF INTEREST

100 BEST-LOVED POEMS, Edited by Philip Smith. "The Passionate Shepherd to His Love," "Shall I compare thee to a summer's day?" "Death, be not proud," "The Raven," "The Road Not Taken," plus works by Blake, Wordsworth, Byron, Shelley, Keats, many others. 96pp. $5\frac{3}{16}$ x $8\frac{1}{4}$. 0-486-28553-7

100 SMALL HOUSES OF THE THIRTIES, Brown-Blodgett Company. Exterior photographs and floor plans for 100 charming structures. Illustrations of models accompanied by descriptions of interiors, color schemes, closet space, and other amenities. 200 illustrations. 112pp. $8\frac{3}{8}$ x 11. 0-486-44131-8

1000 TURN-OF-THE-CENTURY HOUSES: With Illustrations and Floor Plans, Herbert C. Chivers. Reproduced from a rare edition, this showcase of homes ranges from cottages and bungalows to sprawling mansions. Each house is meticulously illustrated and accompanied by complete floor plans. 256pp. $9\frac{3}{8}$ x $12\frac{1}{4}$. 0-486-45596-3

101 GREAT AMERICAN POEMS, Edited by The American Poetry & Literacy Project. Rich treasury of verse from the 19th and 20th centuries includes works by Edgar Allan Poe, Robert Frost, Walt Whitman, Langston Hughes, Emily Dickinson, T. S. Eliot, other notables. 96pp. $5\frac{3}{16}$ x $8\frac{1}{4}$. 0-486-40158-8

101 GREAT SAMURAI PRINTS, Utagawa Kuniyoshi. Kuniyoshi was a master of the warrior woodblock print — and these 18th-century illustrations represent the pinnacle of his craft. Full-color portraits of renowned Japanese samurais pulse with movement, passion, and remarkably fine detail. 112pp. $8\frac{3}{8}$ x 11. 0-486-46523-3

ABC OF BALLET, Janet Grosser. Clearly worded, abundantly illustrated little guide defines basic ballet-related terms: arabesque, battement, pas de chat, relevé, sissonne, many others. Pronunciation guide included. Excellent primer. 48pp. $4\frac{3}{16}$ x $5\frac{3}{4}$. 0-486-40871-X

ACCESSORIES OF DRESS: An Illustrated Encyclopedia, Katherine Lester and Bess Viola Oerke. Illustrations of hats, veils, wigs, cravats, shawls, shoes, gloves, and other accessories enhance an engaging commentary that reveals the humor and charm of the many-sided story of accessorized apparel. 644 figures and 59 plates. 608pp. $6\frac{1}{8}$ x $9\frac{1}{4}$. 0-486-43378-1

ADVENTURES OF HUCKLEBERRY FINN, Mark Twain. Join Huck and Jim as their boyhood adventures along the Mississippi River lead them into a world of excitement, danger, and self-discovery. Humorous narrative, lyrical descriptions of the Mississippi valley, and memorable characters. 224pp. $5\frac{3}{16}$ x $8\frac{1}{4}$. 0-486-28061-6

ALICE STARMORE'S BOOK OF FAIR ISLE KNITTING, Alice Starmore. A noted designer from the region of Scotland's Fair Isle explores the history and techniques of this distinctive, stranded-color knitting style and provides copious illustrated instructions for 14 original knitwear designs. 208pp. $8\frac{3}{8}$ x $10\frac{7}{8}$. 0-486-47218-3

Browse over 9,000 books at www.doverpublications.com

THE BATTLES THAT CHANGED HISTORY, Fletcher Pratt. Historian profiles 16 crucial conflicts, ancient to modern, that changed the course of Western civilization. Gripping accounts of battles led by Alexander the Great, Joan of Arc, Ulysses S. Grant, other commanders. 27 maps. 352pp. 5⅜ x 8½. 0-486-41129-X

BEETHOVEN'S LETTERS, Ludwig van Beethoven. Edited by Dr. A. C. Kalischer. Features 457 letters to fellow musicians, friends, greats, patrons, and literary men. Reveals musical thoughts, quirks of personality, insights, and daily events. Includes 15 plates. 410pp. 5⅜ x 8½. 0-486-22769-3

BERNICE BOBS HER HAIR AND OTHER STORIES, F. Scott Fitzgerald. This brilliant anthology includes 6 of Fitzgerald's most popular stories: "The Diamond as Big as the Ritz," the title tale, "The Offshore Pirate," "The Ice Palace," "The Jelly Bean," and "May Day." 176pp. 5⅜ x 8½. 0-486-47049-0

BESLER'S BOOK OF FLOWERS AND PLANTS: 73 Full-Color Plates from Hortus Eystettensis, 1613, Basilius Besler. Here is a selection of magnificent plates from the *Hortus Eystettensis,* which vividly illustrated and identified the plants, flowers, and trees that thrived in the legendary German garden at Eichstätt. 80pp. 8⅜ x 11. 0-486-46005-3

THE BOOK OF KELLS, Edited by Blanche Cirker. Painstakingly reproduced from a rare facsimile edition, this volume contains full-page decorations, portraits, illustrations, plus a sampling of textual leaves with exquisite calligraphy and ornamentation. 32 full-color illustrations. 32pp. 9⅜ x 12¼. 0-486-24345-1

THE BOOK OF THE CROSSBOW: With an Additional Section on Catapults and Other Siege Engines, Ralph Payne-Gallwey. Fascinating study traces history and use of crossbow as military and sporting weapon, from Middle Ages to modern times. Also covers related weapons: balistas, catapults, Turkish bows, more. Over 240 illustrations. 400pp. 7¼ x 10⅛. 0-486-28720-3

THE BUNGALOW BOOK: Floor Plans and Photos of 112 Houses, 1910, Henry L. Wilson. Here are 112 of the most popular and economic blueprints of the early 20th century — plus an illustration or photograph of each completed house. A wonderful time capsule that still offers a wealth of valuable insights. 160pp. 8⅜ x 11. 0-486-45104-6

THE CALL OF THE WILD, Jack London. A classic novel of adventure, drawn from London's own experiences as a Klondike adventurer, relating the story of a heroic dog caught in the brutal life of the Alaska Gold Rush. Note. 64pp. 5³⁄₁₆ x 8¼. 0-486-26472-6

CANDIDE, Voltaire. Edited by Francois-Marie Arouet. One of the world's great satires since its first publication in 1759. Witty, caustic skewering of romance, science, philosophy, religion, government — nearly all human ideals and institutions. 112pp. 5³⁄₁₆ x 8¼. 0-486-26689-3

CELEBRATED IN THEIR TIME: Photographic Portraits from the George Grantham Bain Collection, Edited by Amy Pastan. With an Introduction by Michael Carlebach. Remarkable portrait gallery features 112 rare images of Albert Einstein, Charlie Chaplin, the Wright Brothers, Henry Ford, and other luminaries from the worlds of politics, art, entertainment, and industry. 128pp. 8⅜ x 11. 0-486-46754-6

CHARIOTS FOR APOLLO: The NASA History of Manned Lunar Spacecraft to 1969, Courtney G. Brooks, James M. Grimwood, and Loyd S. Swenson, Jr. This illustrated history by a trio of experts is the definitive reference on the Apollo spacecraft and lunar modules. It traces the vehicles' design, development, and operation in space. More than 100 photographs and illustrations. 576pp. 6¾ x 9¼. 0-486-46756-2

DOOMED SHIPS: Great Ocean Liner Disasters, William H. Miller, Jr. Nearly 200 photographs, many from private collections, highlight tales of some of the vessels whose pleasure cruises ended in catastrophe: the *Morro Castle, Normandie, Andrea Doria, Europa,* and many others. 128pp. $8\frac{7}{8}$ x $11\frac{3}{4}$. 0-486-45366-9

THE DORÉ BIBLE ILLUSTRATIONS, Gustave Doré. Detailed plates from the Bible: the Creation scenes, Adam and Eve, horrifying visions of the Flood, the battle sequences with their monumental crowds, depictions of the life of Jesus, 241 plates in all. 241pp. 9 x 12. 0-486-23004-X

DRAWING DRAPERY FROM HEAD TO TOE, Cliff Young. Expert guidance on how to draw shirts, pants, skirts, gloves, hats, and coats on the human figure, including folds in relation to the body, pull and crush, action folds, creases, more. Over 200 drawings. 48pp. $8\frac{1}{4}$ x 11. 0-486-45591-2

DUBLINERS, James Joyce. A fine and accessible introduction to the work of one of the 20th century's most influential writers, this collection features 15 tales, including a masterpiece of the short-story genre, "The Dead." 160pp. $5\frac{3}{16}$ x $8\frac{1}{4}$. 0-486-26870-5

EASY-TO-MAKE POP-UPS, Joan Irvine. Illustrated by Barbara Reid. Dozens of wonderful ideas for three-dimensional paper fun — from holiday greeting cards with moving parts to a pop-up menagerie. Easy-to-follow, illustrated instructions for more than 30 projects. 299 black-and-white illustrations. 96pp. $8\frac{3}{8}$ x 11. 0-486-44622-0

EASY-TO-MAKE STORYBOOK DOLLS: A "Novel" Approach to Cloth Dollmaking, Sherralyn St. Clair. Favorite fictional characters come alive in this unique beginner's dollmaking guide. Includes patterns for Pollyanna, Dorothy from *The Wonderful Wizard of Oz,* Mary of *The Secret Garden,* plus easy-to-follow instructions, 263 black-and-white illustrations, and an 8-page color insert. 112pp. $8\frac{1}{4}$ x 11. 0-486-47360-0

EINSTEIN'S ESSAYS IN SCIENCE, Albert Einstein. Speeches and essays in accessible, everyday language profile influential physicists such as Niels Bohr and Isaac Newton. They also explore areas of physics to which the author made major contributions. 128pp. 5 x 8. 0-486-47011-3

EL DORADO: Further Adventures of the Scarlet Pimpernel, Baroness Orczy. A popular sequel to *The Scarlet Pimpernel,* this suspenseful story recounts the Pimpernel's attempts to rescue the Dauphin from imprisonment during the French Revolution. An irresistible blend of intrigue, period detail, and vibrant characterizations. 352pp. $5\frac{3}{16}$ x $8\frac{1}{4}$. 0-486-44026-5

ELEGANT SMALL HOMES OF THE TWENTIES: 99 Designs from a Competition, Chicago Tribune. Nearly 100 designs for five- and six-room houses feature New England and Southern colonials, Normandy cottages, stately Italianate dwellings, and other fascinating snapshots of American domestic architecture of the 1920s. 112pp. 9 x 12. 0-486-46910-7

THE ELEMENTS OF STYLE: The Original Edition, William Strunk, Jr. This is the book that generations of writers have relied upon for timeless advice on grammar, diction, syntax, and other essentials. In concise terms, it identifies the principal requirements of proper style and common errors. 64pp. $5\frac{3}{8}$ x $8\frac{1}{2}$. 0-486-44798-7

THE ELUSIVE PIMPERNEL, Baroness Orczy. Robespierre's revolutionaries find their wicked schemes thwarted by the heroic Pimpernel — Sir Percival Blakeney. In this thrilling sequel, Chauvelin devises a plot to eliminate the Pimpernel and his wife. 272pp. $5\frac{3}{16}$ x $8\frac{1}{4}$. 0-486-45464-9

AN ENCYCLOPEDIA OF BATTLES: Accounts of Over 1,560 Battles from 1479 B.C. to the Present, David Eggenberger. Essential details of every major battle in recorded history from the first battle of Megiddo in 1479 B.C. to Grenada in 1984. List of battle maps. 99 illustrations. 544pp. 6½ x 9¼. 0-486-24913-1

ENCYCLOPEDIA OF EMBROIDERY STITCHES, INCLUDING CREWEL, Marion Nichols. Precise explanations and instructions, clearly illustrated, on how to work chain, back, cross, knotted, woven stitches, and many more — 178 in all, including Cable Outline, Whipped Satin, and Eyelet Buttonhole. Over 1400 illustrations. 219pp. 8⅜ x 11¼. 0-486-22929-7

ENTER JEEVES: 15 Early Stories, P. G. Wodehouse. Splendid collection contains first 8 stories featuring Bertie Wooster, the deliciously dim aristocrat and Jeeves, his brainy, imperturbable manservant. Also, the complete Reggie Pepper (Bertie's prototype) series. 288pp. 5⅜ x 8½. 0-486-29717-9

ERIC SLOANE'S AMERICA: Paintings in Oil, Michael Wigley. With a Foreword by Mimi Sloane. Eric Sloane's evocative oils of America's landscape and material culture shimmer with immense historical and nostalgic appeal. This original hardcover collection gathers nearly a hundred of his finest paintings, with subjects ranging from New England to the American Southwest. 128pp. 10⅝ x 9. 0-486-46525-X

ETHAN FROME, Edith Wharton. Classic story of wasted lives, set against a bleak New England background. Superbly delineated characters in a hauntingly grim tale of thwarted love. Considered by many to be Wharton's masterpiece. 96pp. 5 3/16 x 8 ¼. 0-486-26690-7

THE EVERLASTING MAN, G. K. Chesterton. Chesterton's view of Christianity — as a blend of philosophy and mythology, satisfying intellect and spirit — applies to his brilliant book, which appeals to readers' heads as well as their hearts. 288pp. 5⅜ x 8½. 0-486-46036-3

THE FIELD AND FOREST HANDY BOOK, Daniel Beard. Written by a co-founder of the Boy Scouts, this appealing guide offers illustrated instructions for building kites, birdhouses, boats, igloos, and other fun projects, plus numerous helpful tips for campers. 448pp. 5 3/16 x 8¼. 0-486-46191-2

FINDING YOUR WAY WITHOUT MAP OR COMPASS, Harold Gatty. Useful, instructive manual shows would-be explorers, hikers, bikers, scouts, sailors, and survivalists how to find their way outdoors by observing animals, weather patterns, shifting sands, and other elements of nature. 288pp. 5⅜ x 8½. 0-486-40613-X

FIRST FRENCH READER: A Beginner's Dual-Language Book, Edited and Translated by Stanley Appelbaum. This anthology introduces 50 legendary writers — Voltaire, Balzac, Baudelaire, Proust, more — through passages from *The Red and the Black, Les Misérables, Madame Bovary,* and other classics. Original French text plus English translation on facing pages. 240pp. 5⅜ x 8½. 0-486-46178-5

FIRST GERMAN READER: A Beginner's Dual-Language Book, Edited by Harry Steinhauer. Specially chosen for their power to evoke German life and culture, these short, simple readings include poems, stories, essays, and anecdotes by Goethe, Hesse, Heine, Schiller, and others. 224pp. 5⅜ x 8½. 0-486-46179-3

FIRST SPANISH READER: A Beginner's Dual-Language Book, Angel Flores. Delightful stories, other material based on works of Don Juan Manuel, Luis Taboada, Ricardo Palma, other noted writers. Complete faithful English translations on facing pages. Exercises. 176pp. 5⅜ x 8½. 0-486-25810-6

THE JUNGLE, Upton Sinclair. 1906 bestseller shockingly reveals intolerable labor practices and working conditions in the Chicago stockyards as it tells the grim story of a Slavic family that emigrates to America full of optimism but soon faces despair. 320pp. 5$\frac{3}{16}$ x 8$\frac{1}{4}$. 0-486-41923-1

THE KINGDOM OF GOD IS WITHIN YOU, Leo Tolstoy. The soul-searching book that inspired Gandhi to embrace the concept of passive resistance, Tolstoy's 1894 polemic clearly outlines a radical, well-reasoned revision of traditional Christian thinking. 352pp. 5$\frac{3}{16}$ x 8$\frac{1}{4}$. 0-486-45138-0

THE LADY OR THE TIGER?: and Other Logic Puzzles, Raymond M. Smullyan. Created by a renowned puzzle master, these whimsically themed challenges involve paradoxes about probability, time, and change; metapuzzles; and self-referentiality. Nineteen chapters advance in difficulty from relatively simple to highly complex. 1982 edition. 240pp. 5$\frac{3}{8}$ x 8$\frac{1}{2}$. 0-486-47027-X

LEAVES OF GRASS: The Original 1855 Edition, Walt Whitman. Whitman's immortal collection includes some of the greatest poems of modern times, including his masterpiece, "Song of Myself." Shattering standard conventions, it stands as an unabashed celebration of body and nature. 128pp. 5$\frac{3}{16}$ x 8$\frac{1}{4}$. 0-486-45676-5

LES MISÉRABLES, Victor Hugo. Translated by Charles E. Wilbour. Abridged by James K. Robinson. A convict's heroic struggle for justice and redemption plays out against a fiery backdrop of the Napoleonic wars. This edition features the excellent original translation and a sensitive abridgment. 304pp. 6$\frac{1}{8}$ x 9$\frac{1}{4}$. 0-486-45789-3

LILITH: A Romance, George MacDonald. In this novel by the father of fantasy literature, a man travels through time to meet Adam and Eve and to explore humanity's fall from grace and ultimate redemption. 240pp. 5$\frac{3}{8}$ x 8$\frac{1}{2}$. 0-486-46818-6

THE LOST LANGUAGE OF SYMBOLISM, Harold Bayley. This remarkable book reveals the hidden meaning behind familiar images and words, from the origins of Santa Claus to the fleur-de-lys, drawing from mythology, folklore, religious texts, and fairy tales. 1,418 illustrations. 784pp. 5$\frac{3}{8}$ x 8$\frac{1}{2}$. 0-486-44787-1

MACBETH, William Shakespeare. A Scottish nobleman murders the king in order to succeed to the throne. Tortured by his conscience and fearful of discovery, he becomes tangled in a web of treachery and deceit that ultimately spells his doom. 96pp. 5$\frac{3}{16}$ x 8$\frac{1}{4}$. 0-486-27802-6

MAKING AUTHENTIC CRAFTSMAN FURNITURE: Instructions and Plans for 62 Projects, Gustav Stickley. Make authentic reproductions of handsome, functional, durable furniture: tables, chairs, wall cabinets, desks, a hall tree, and more. Construction plans with drawings, schematics, dimensions, and lumber specs reprinted from 1900s *The Craftsman* magazine. 128pp. 8$\frac{1}{8}$ x 11. 0-486-25000-8

MATHEMATICS FOR THE NONMATHEMATICIAN, Morris Kline. Erudite and entertaining overview follows development of mathematics from ancient Greeks to present. Topics include logic and mathematics, the fundamental concept, differential calculus, probability theory, much more. Exercises and problems. 641pp. 5$\frac{3}{8}$ x 8$\frac{1}{2}$. 0-486-24823-2

MEMOIRS OF AN ARABIAN PRINCESS FROM ZANZIBAR, Emily Ruete. This 19th-century autobiography offers a rare inside look at the society surrounding a sultan's palace. A real-life princess in exile recalls her vanished world of harems, slave trading, and court intrigues. 288pp. 5$\frac{3}{8}$ x 8$\frac{1}{2}$. 0-486-47121-7

CATALOG OF DOVER BOOKS

THE METAMORPHOSIS AND OTHER STORIES, Franz Kafka. Excellent new English translations of title story (considered by many critics Kafka's most perfect work), plus "The Judgment," "In the Penal Colony," "A Country Doctor," and "A Report to an Academy." Note. 96pp. 5$\frac{3}{16}$ x 8$\frac{1}{4}$. 0-486-29030-1

MICROSCOPIC ART FORMS FROM THE PLANT WORLD, R. Anheisser. From undulating curves to complex geometrics, a world of fascinating images abound in this classic, illustrated survey of microscopic plants. Features 400 detailed illustrations of nature's minute but magnificent handiwork. The accompanying CD-ROM includes all of the images in the book. 128pp. 9 x 9. 0-486-46013-4

A MIDSUMMER NIGHT'S DREAM, William Shakespeare. Among the most popular of Shakespeare's comedies, this enchanting play humorously celebrates the vagaries of love as it focuses upon the intertwined romances of several pairs of lovers. Explanatory footnotes. 80pp. 5$\frac{3}{16}$ x 8$\frac{1}{4}$. 0-486-27067-X

THE MONEY CHANGERS, Upton Sinclair. Originally published in 1908, this cautionary novel from the author of *The Jungle* explores corruption within the American system as a group of power brokers joins forces for personal gain, triggering a crash on Wall Street. 192pp. 5$\frac{3}{8}$ x 8$\frac{1}{2}$. 0-486-46917-4

THE MOST POPULAR HOMES OF THE TWENTIES, William A. Radford. With a New Introduction by Daniel D. Reiff. Based on a rare 1925 catalog, this architectural showcase features floor plans, construction details, and photos of 26 homes, plus articles on entrances, porches, garages, and more. 250 illustrations, 21 color plates. 176pp. 8$\frac{3}{8}$ x 11. 0-486-47028-8

MY 66 YEARS IN THE BIG LEAGUES, Connie Mack. With a New Introduction by Rich Westcott. A Founding Father of modern baseball, Mack holds the record for most wins — and losses — by a major league manager. Enhanced by 70 photographs, his warmhearted autobiography is populated by many legends of the game. 288pp. 5$\frac{3}{8}$ x 8$\frac{1}{2}$. 0-486-47184-5

NARRATIVE OF THE LIFE OF FREDERICK DOUGLASS, Frederick Douglass. Douglass's graphic depictions of slavery, harrowing escape to freedom, and life as a newspaper editor, eloquent orator, and impassioned abolitionist. 96pp. 5$\frac{3}{16}$ x 8$\frac{1}{4}$. 0-486-28499-9

THE NIGHTLESS CITY: Geisha and Courtesan Life in Old Tokyo, J. E. de Becker. This unsurpassed study from 100 years ago ventured into Tokyo's red-light district to survey geisha and courtesan life and offer meticulous descriptions of training, dress, social hierarchy, and erotic practices. 49 black-and-white illustrations; 2 maps. 496pp. 5$\frac{3}{8}$ x 8$\frac{1}{2}$. 0-486-45563-7

THE ODYSSEY, Homer. Excellent prose translation of ancient epic recounts adventures of the homeward-bound Odysseus. Fantastic cast of gods, giants, cannibals, sirens, other supernatural creatures — true classic of Western literature. 256pp. 5$\frac{3}{16}$ x 8$\frac{1}{4}$. 0-486-40654-7

OEDIPUS REX, Sophocles. Landmark of Western drama concerns the catastrophe that ensues when King Oedipus discovers he has inadvertently killed his father and married his mother. Masterly construction, dramatic irony. Explanatory footnotes. 64pp. 5$\frac{3}{16}$ x 8$\frac{1}{4}$. 0-486-26877-2

ONCE UPON A TIME: The Way America Was, Eric Sloane. Nostalgic text and drawings brim with gentle philosophies and descriptions of how we used to live — self-sufficiently — on the land, in homes, and among the things built by hand. 44 line illustrations. 64pp. 8$\frac{3}{8}$ x 11. 0-486-44411-2

THE TRIAL, Franz Kafka. Translated by David Wyllie. From its gripping first sentence onward, this novel exemplifies the term "Kafkaesque." Its darkly humorous narrative recounts a bank clerk's entrapment in a bureaucratic maze, based on an undisclosed charge. 176pp. $5\frac{3}{16}$ x $8\frac{1}{4}$. 0-486-47061-X

THE TURN OF THE SCREW, Henry James. Gripping ghost story by great novelist depicts the sinister transformation of 2 innocent children into flagrant liars and hypocrites. An elegantly told tale of unspoken horror and psychological terror. 96pp. $5\frac{3}{16}$ x $8\frac{1}{4}$. 0-486-26684-2

UP FROM SLAVERY, Booker T. Washington. Washington (1856-1915) rose to become the most influential spokesman for African-Americans of his day. In this eloquently written book, he describes events in a remarkable life that began in bondage and culminated in worldwide recognition. 160pp. $5\frac{3}{16}$ x $8\frac{1}{4}$. 0-486-28738-6

VICTORIAN HOUSE DESIGNS IN AUTHENTIC FULL COLOR: 75 Plates from the "Scientific American – Architects and Builders Edition," 1885-1894, Edited by Blanche Cirker. Exquisitely detailed, exceptionally handsome designs for an enormous variety of attractive city dwellings, spacious suburban and country homes, charming "cottages" and other structures — all accompanied by perspective views and floor plans. 80pp. $9\frac{1}{4}$ x $12\frac{1}{4}$. 0-486-29438-2

VILLETTE, Charlotte Brontë. Acclaimed by Virginia Woolf as "Brontë's finest novel," this moving psychological study features a remarkably modern heroine who abandons her native England for a new life as a schoolteacher in Belgium. 480pp. $5\frac{3}{16}$ x $8\frac{1}{4}$. 0-486-45557-2

THE VOYAGE OUT, Virginia Woolf. A moving depiction of the thrills and confusion of youth, Woolf's acclaimed first novel traces a shipboard journey to South America for a captivating exploration of a woman's growing self-awareness. 288pp. $5\frac{3}{16}$ x $8\frac{1}{4}$. 0-486-45005-8

WALDEN; OR, LIFE IN THE WOODS, Henry David Thoreau. Accounts of Thoreau's daily life on the shores of Walden Pond outside Concord, Massachusetts, are interwoven with musings on the virtues of self-reliance and individual freedom, on society, government, and other topics. 224pp. $5\frac{3}{16}$ x $8\frac{1}{4}$. 0-486-28495-6

WILD PILGRIMAGE: A Novel in Woodcuts, Lynd Ward. Through startling engravings shaded in black and red, Ward wordlessly tells the story of a man trapped in an industrial world, struggling between the grim reality around him and the fantasies his imagination creates. 112pp. $6\frac{1}{8}$ x $9\frac{1}{4}$. 0-486-46583-7

WILLY POGÁNY REDISCOVERED, Willy Pogány. Selected and Edited by Jeff A. Menges. More than 100 color and black-and-white Art Nouveau–style illustrations from fairy tales and adventure stories include scenes from Wagner's "Ring" cycle, *The Rime of the Ancient Mariner, Gulliver's Travels,* and *Faust.* 144pp. $8\frac{3}{8}$ x 11. 0-486-47046-6

WOOLLY THOUGHTS: Unlock Your Creative Genius with Modular Knitting, Pat Ashforth and Steve Plummer. Here's the revolutionary way to knit — easy, fun, and foolproof! Beginners and experienced knitters need only master a single stitch to create their own designs with patchwork squares. More than 100 illustrations. 128pp. $6\frac{1}{2}$ x $9\frac{1}{4}$. 0-486-46084-3

WUTHERING HEIGHTS, Emily Brontë. Somber tale of consuming passions and vengeance — played out amid the lonely English moors — recounts the turbulent and tempestuous love story of Cathy and Heathcliff. Poignant and compelling. 256pp. $5\frac{3}{16}$ x $8\frac{1}{4}$. 0-486-29256-8